T|
Spirit

By Hugh Morrison

MONTPELIER PUBLISHING
2025

© Hugh Morrison 2025

All rights reserved. No part of this publication may be reproduced, stored in a retrieval system, or transmitted, in any form or by any means without the prior written permission of the publisher, nor be otherwise circulated in any form of binding or cover other than that in which it is published and without a similar condition including this condition being imposed on the subsequent purchaser.

Published in Great Britain by Montpelier Publishing.
www.hughmorrisonbooks.com
Set in Palatino Linotype 11 point
Cover image by Miguna Studio
ISBN: 9798316517763

 Follow Montpelier Publishing on Facebook

Chapter One

The Honourable Eleanor Harrington was prepared to kill.

She hoped she would not have to, but it seemed to her that killing those whom she believed intended to kill her was a justified form of self-defence, in moral if not perhaps strictly legal terms.

She looked out of the barred window at the gathering dusk in the garden; without a watch or a clock it was hard to know the exact time, but she could reasonably guess to within half an hour or so. Between five thirty and six pm. The nurse would be here soon. Would there be a chance today?

The electric light, high up in the ceiling behind a metal grille, suddenly flicked on. It was controlled from outside, and that meant the nurse was about to enter. At this time of year it was dark by six and so the light turned the barred window of the room into a mirror. Mirrors, of course, were not allowed; they could be easily broken and turned into a makeshift weapon.

She caught sight of herself in the window. Lord, what a fright, she thought. Hair cropped short in an amateurish bob, and of course not a bit of makeup. The coarse, institutional frock that doubled as a nightie and hung off her shapelessly. She was still young, though, and had a good bone structure and clear skin, although it was bleached pale by spending too much time indoors. Ah well, she thought, just one more reason to get out of this damned place; how she longed for a proper hairdresser and a manicure!

The door was unlocked, and in bustled Reeves, the nurse. The Harridan, as Eleanor thought of her. She had probably been moderately attractive, once, but was now middle aged and hatchet-faced. One of those self-important charitable types who are always serving on committees and interfering in other people's business. She wore a dowdy uniform and spoke in one of those posh-common accents that functionaries use in the hope of sounding important.

'How are we today, Miss Harrington?' said the nurse brightly as she jangled her keys and balanced them on the metal tray bearing a metal cup full of water and a metal plate with two large black pills on it.

The nurse had at first adopted a jocular form of address, calling Eleanor 'your ladyship', until Eleanor had told her not to be so damned stupid and to find a book of etiquette if she didn't know how to address the daughter of a Baron. That had put the silly woman in her place, thought Eleanor with a smile, and also seemed to have gained her a new-found respect.

Since then, the nurse had spoken to her in a more friendly manner, chattering away to her about all sorts of things that she assumed were of interest but which to Eleanor sounded inconceivably dull.

'No…worse than…usual,' said Eleanor slowly, forcing herself not to sound too coherent. She was careful not to overdo it, and make herself sound like a drooling idiot, as that might attract suspicion also.

'Jolly good,' said the nurse blandly. 'One needs three hands in this job. I've got my bally key chain all tangled with the side of this tray. Shan't be a moment.'

Eleanor watched as the woman put the metal tray down on the wooden table which stood, securely bolted into the floor, in a corner of the room. 'Now then, that's better,' she said, releasing the key chain from her uniform belt and placing the large bunch next to the tray.

'I get so mixed up with all these keys!' she exclaimed brightly. 'I know the one with the black fob is for my motor car, and the biggest one is for the front door, but as for the others, well, I haven't a clue, so I've had to label them all!'

That blasted motor car again, thought Eleanor. The woman couldn't stop showing off about it, how it was brand new, how long she'd had to save up for it, and how easy it was to start, unlike the older cars that needed a starting handle. The woman acted as if having a car were the be all and end all. Eleanor, however, had two older brothers who had always been messing about with motor cars and she had learned to drive at the age of eleven on her family estate. The subject held very little interest for her.

'Now then,' said the nurse, lifting up the metal plate with its two unpleasant looking pills on it. 'Down the hatch, please.'

'Don't...want to...' slurred Eleanor sullenly.

'We'll have no fuss,' said Reeves. 'I've told you I went to a lot of trouble to get Dr Landis to agree to oral medication instead of intravenous, because I could tell you didn't like needles. You don't want to have to go back to that, do you?'

Eleanor shuddered. How long had she been in that dream world from those injections? Weeks, perhaps months? And then they had changed it to pills, which seemed slightly less effective and had allowed her moments of mental clarity. It was during those moments she had formulated her plan.

For a week now she had not taken any medication. She had noticed, while spending long hours gazing out of the window of her room into the garden, that the window frame (locked, of course, and containing reinforced glass which could not be broken) was lined with black mould where the frames had begun to rot. She had carefully scooped some of this substance off, and rolled it around in her fingers, realising she could make a pill shaped object that was almost indistinguishable from the real thing once it had dried.

At first she wondered if it might be harmful to ingest it; wasn't black mould supposed to be bad for the chest, or something? She laughed to herself; it couldn't be worse than the filth in those pills they forced her to take.

When she first tried the substitution her hands were trembling, but the nurse must have put this down to her drug-addled state, and she didn't seem to notice anything awry. Eleanor had been practicing the sleight of hand required to swap the mould-pills with the real thing, dropping them up her sleeve in the way she remembered her brother Clive showing her after he had received an amateur conjuring set for Christmas.

Reeves, as usual, had given her a beaker of water and after she drank, had made her open her mouth and inspected it like a dentist, to make sure the pills were not concealed under her tongue. The ruse seemed to have worked. After each deception, the real pills were simply left to dissolve in the slop-bucket in the corner, and that was that.

Each day she felt her mental clarity returning, like sunlight gradually clearing away the morning mist, and each day she planned out in her mind just how she was going to escape.

The pill routine successfully executed again, the nurse crossed to the window and looked out. Would she notice the missing mould?, thought Eleanor in a sudden moment of panic. She had been careful to scrape it evenly. Even if she did notice, surely she wouldn't put two and two together?

Eleanor breathed a small sigh of relief as she realised the woman wasn't in the slightest bit interested in the window frame.

'There's my pride and joy,' she said. 'I always park it in the same place, under that pine on the side of the drive, because the birds don't seem to like it there and it keeps the mess off.'

Eleanor felt her heart begin pounding in her chest. If this wasn't a chance, then what would be? The mould was nearly all gone from the window frame now...and there were the keys on the table, disconnected from the nurse's belt. Because the stupid woman wouldn't stop prattling, Eleanor now knew which keys were which, and what was more, she knew exactly where the car was parked.

In one of those moments where reason seems to be completely excluded by a pure urge for action, Eleanor seized the heavy metal tray from the table and drove the edge of it brutally onto the side of Reeves' head. She expected a huge crash and a scream, but none came; instead the woman simply groaned and collapsed face down on to the linoleum.

For a brief moment Eleanor thought she was dead, and her former resolve to kill if necessary was replaced by something approaching pity; the natural concern of a civilized human being for another's welfare, even if that were one's enemy. She felt a moment of relief as she realised the woman was still breathing. There was no time for sentiment; she had to act – now.

She pulled off the woman's uniform coat and wide-brimmed hat; Eleanor's room was the last on her rounds before she went home and she had usually put it on by the time she called. Eleanor then pulled off the nurse's shoes and shoved them on to her own feet, wincing as the tight leather cut in to her. They were too small, but they would have to do.

She rolled up the hem of her dress so that it didn't show; hopefully nobody would notice her lack of stockings under the long coat; there was no time to remove those of the unconscious nurse.

Picking up the large bunch of keys she moved to the door; she realised she did not know which key opened it. She fumbled through the assortment with mounting panic, but then stopped. The stupid woman had not even locked the door behind her! Gingerly she tried the heavy metal handle and the door creaked open.

She stepped out into the dimly-lit corridor and looked up and down; nobody about. Keeping her head down, her face obscured by the unflattering nurse's hat, she soon reached the front hallway, her heart pounding in her chest. As she had feared, there was a man sitting at the heavy mahogany desk by the door, reading a newspaper. It was one of the orderlies, the one that looked like he was not far off being a mental case himself. Barton. Yes, that was his name. Heavily built with a look of vacant anger in his eyes, always ready to be more firm than needed when restraint was called for, as if he relished the act of control. She kept her head down and hurried to the door.

She could feel Barton's eyes on her as she fumbled with the bunch of keys, forcing herself to keep calm as she looked for the largest one, as Reeves had mentioned. Finally she found it and slipped it into the heavy lock. It refused to turn.

'Just a minute,' said Barton from behind her.

This was it, thought Eleanor. Well, it had been a good try. Expecting to feel Barton's ape-like hands seize her arms in a vice-like grip, she was surprised to feel him gently place his hand over hers and twist it firmly, allowing the key to turn.

'Sticking a bit today,' he said. 'Must need a bit of oil, I daresay.'

Keeping her head down, Eleanor merely nodded and sharply pulled the door open.

'Well, cheer-oh, miss,' said Barton. 'See you tomorrow.'

Eleanor grunted non-committally, trying to pitch the sound at the level of the nurse's voice; she dared not attempt any closer imitation.

She stepped forward onto the large stone porch of the old house, and heard the door clang shut behind her. She could barely believe it – she was almost free! But not quite – there was still the man at the gate to get past.

She looked at the row of vehicles to the left of the house; there was the large, expensive car belonging to Dr Landis, a couple of decrepit 'flivvers' and a motorcycle combination belonging to the orderlies, and the nurse's Wolseley. She knew it was hers because of its colour, a bright shade which the nurse had proudly described as being called Tropic Green.

How long had she got?, she wondered. Surely any moment the nurse would regain consciousness and sound the alarm. She suddenly realised she ought to have locked Reeves in, but it was too late now. She must get into the car!

The moon had now risen, and there was just light enough for her to make out the key fob for the car; she unlocked the door and slid into the driver's seat. She looked at the controls rapidly; it was rather different to the old wrecks she had driven with her brothers at home, but the principle was the same. Yes, there it was, just as the nurse had said; a keyhole and next to it a white button marked 'starter'. She turned the key in the lock and pressed the button. Nothing happened.

Frantically she turned the key back and forth and this time, it seemed to go further to the right than before. She pressed the starter again, and the engine roared into life. She switched the headlamps on and then looked down at her feet; accelerator, footbrake, clutch; yes it was all the same.

She squinted at the little diagram on the gear lever and tried to remember the process of double-declutching as she grasped it; she pressed the clutch and there was an unhealthy metallic crunching sound.

'Oh *please* work, you beastly thing...' she cried out in frustration.

As if the engine could hear her command, it slipped into gear and the car lurched forward. She managed to engage reverse and then turned to face the front gate. In the glare of the powerful headlamps she saw the other orderly come out of the little lodge by the gate. Had she been detected? No! He was opening the gates!

She drove forward slowly, confident that the man could not see her face due to the headlamps shining on him. He slowly opened one of the gates, and then moved to the other. Then he stopped, and looked towards the house.

Eleanor glanced in the rear view mirror and saw that the front door of the house was open, and figures were running toward her. Over the noise of the engine she realised she could hear the insistent sound of an electric alarm bell, and intermittent shouting.

Without any pause for thought, Eleanor slammed her foot on the accelerator and the car surged forward, its powerful engine building speed more rapidly than she expected. The orderly paused momentarily, as if he were working out his chances of getting the gate closed in time, then he gave up the idea and leapt to one side. There was an enormous crash as the passenger side of the car hit the half open gate, shattering one of the headlamps and shearing off the mudguard as it went, but the car got through.

Eleanor wrestled with the steering wheel as the car shimmied over the patch of muddy ground between the gate and the road, and then she veered to the right. The ride suddenly became smoother, and she realised she was on a metalled road. She was free!

She breathed deeply and tried to regain her composure, but in the process, could not help but allow herself a laugh of triumph. But then she looked in the rear view mirror.

She was being followed. A car had turned out of the house's driveway and was now a few hundred yards behind her. She pressed harder on the accelerator, squinting at the road which was only sparsely lit by the car's one remaining headlamp.

The car picked up speed, but at the same time, seemed to lose its ability to hold to the road; it wobbled and jerked, and it was all Eleanor could do to keep the steering wheel in a straight line. Something must have happened to the mechanism in the collision with the gate, she realised. Would it still get her to London, as she had hoped?

She glanced behind her once more; the car, though still some way back, was gaining ground. She saw up ahead the lights of houses, and the dim outline of a church tower against the moon. A village. Could she get help there?

Before she could consider the matter further, she felt the steering wheel buck wildly, and it momentarily leapt out of her hands. The car lurched to one side and there was a horrific screeching sound and a shower of sparks flew up as if someone had lit a bonfire night catherine wheel under the car. The wheel, she realised, had come off! At that moment she lost all control of the vehicle and it skidded off the road. The last thing she saw before she lost consciousness was the bright white outline of a silver birch tree, and then all was dark.

The Reverend Lucian Shaw, vicar of All Saints' church in the village of Lower Addenham in Suffolk, sat back with an air of complete satisfaction.

'A splendid meal, Mrs Keating,' he said to the woman next to him. 'A remarkable achievement without any servants.'

Alice Keating blushed. She was not exactly a pretty woman, but had a healthy countrywoman's face and was entirely devoid of artfulness or 'airs and graces.'

'You're very kind, vicar,' she said. 'We haven't managed to find anybody yet, apart from Mrs Thewlis who does for us twice a week. All the young girls seem to disappear off to Midchester as soon as they are able.'

'You can hardly blame them,' said the woman opposite Shaw. It was Shaw's wife, Marion, a woman of unvarnished appearance whose face bore the shrewd expression of someone used to dealing with all sorts and conditions of men. 'The new wireless factory there pays far higher wages than anyone here is likely to give them as domestic servants.'

'Oh I don't blame them, Mrs Shaw,' said Mrs Keating. 'I can hardly do that when the man I married moved away himself to find work. And he came all the way from Ireland.'

Dr Patrick Keating looked at his wife from his place at the head of the table in the small dining room of the little Georgian house which doubled as his home and his surgery. Although not yet forty, his hair was streaked with grey and he had the distinctive hawk-like features bred from generations of Anglo-Irish gentry.

'And it was worth it, my dear, if only because I found such a rare prize as you,' he said to his wife in that romantic Hibernian manner that can move the coldest of English women to girlish blushes.

'I understand you are to be the board doctor for the village,' said Shaw. 'That is excellent news. Until now the nearest such physician for those unable to pay was in Great Netley, and he often refuses to make house calls this far away.'

'Now don't make me out to be some sort of saint just because I take on patients that are funded by the British taxpayer rather than from their own pocket,' said Keating. 'I had to do that to get established here. Once I've been here a while I'll be picking up the filthy rich carriage trade, you just watch me.'

Shaw chuckled. He knew enough about the man already to know he would be a great help to the poor of the village who had to rely on state medical assistance. The village's only other doctor was now elderly, and did little more than attend to the largely imaginary ailments of the local wealthy elite.

There had been some mistrust at first; Keating was assumed to be a Roman Catholic and perhaps even a Fenian, but his regular presence at Shaw's church had allayed such fears, and he was now firmly established as one of the 'characters' of the public bar at the George Inn.

'And now Mr Shaw,' said the physician, 'perhaps the ladies can retire somewhere while we have a drop of the water of life and put this sorry world to rights.'

'Very well, dear,' said Mrs Keating, standing up. 'Now you come with me, Mrs Shaw, and I'll show you into the sitting room and we'll let the men tell their silly stories. Putting the world to rights, indeed.' She ruffled her husband's hair and turned to the door. From outside came the jangle of the front door bell.

'No rest for the wicked,' said Dr Keating with a sigh. 'That'll be Jepson from End Cottage about the baby. I told him to fetch me when it was time. The new midwife's a bit nervous so I offered to help. Alice my dear, fetch Mr Shaw a glass of whiskey, and one for Mrs Shaw if she wants one. It's Mrs Jepson's sixth, so I doubt I'll be long.'

Keating left the dining room door ajar and crossed to the front door, pausing to pat Fraser, Shaw's West Highland terrier, who had been given his own dinner in the hallway. The dog was looking at the front door with great interest and he barked twice, loudly.

'Now don't you be rude to Jepson, wee fellow,' admonished Keating. 'He's a rat-catcher by trade, and it's likely all you're smelling is the scent of the little beggars still on his trousers.'

The bell rang again, more insistently this time.

'All right, I'm on my way,' said the doctor, opening the door. He paused, realising it was not the sizeable farm-hand he had been expecting. Instead, it was a young, tall, rather attractive looking woman dressed in an institutional looking hat and coat. He noticed immediately that she had a swelling bruise on her forehead and had no stockings on her legs.

The woman gave a nervous smile. 'I'm so sorry to bother you. My car's broken down and I wondered if I might use your telephone.'

'Of course,' said Keating, opening the door wide. 'Go to your master,' he said to Fraser, who was sniffing the woman's shoes with interest. 'Go on boy.'

Fraser pattered away into the dining room and Keating gestured into the hallway. 'The telephone's there, on the table. There's some numbers on the pad there. The local garage will be closed by now but Reynolds in Great Netley will be open.'

'Thank you,' said the woman, crossing to the telephone table. She looked down at the pad. 'Netley 312?'

'I think so, yes,' said Keating, regarding her with interest.

'Would you mind shutting the front door?' asked the woman in a tone which suggested she was used to being obeyed. 'I'm afraid I've been stranded for a while and I'm rather feeling the cold.'

'Yes of course,' said Keating, obeying the request. Then the woman turned her back on him and picked up the receiver. Keating noticed, as she did so, some marks on her wrist and arm that reminded him of something from his past. She asked for the number and then had a brief conversation.

'Everything all right?' asked Keating when she had replaced the receiver.

'Yes, quite,' said the woman with a brittle brightness. 'Although he said it might be some time until he can come. An hour, perhaps. I wondered if…'

'Why certainly,' said Keating with a smile. 'Stay as long as you wish, within reason. I'm guessing you're a wee bit hungry, too?'

'Well I must admit I am rather…'

The front door bell jangled again.

'Excuse me a moment,' said Keating, and turned towards the entrance.

'Don't open it!' hissed the woman urgently.

Keating noticed a look of terror had crossed her face, and her hands were shaking. Fraser trotted out of the dining room and faced the front door, a low growl emanating from his throat.

'Stop that noise, Fraser,' ordered Keating, then turned to the woman. There was clearly something wrong with her, and he now wondered if had been right to allow her in. 'It's perfectly all right, just a patient calling,' said Keating. 'I'm a doctor, you see.'

The woman's eyes widened. 'A…doctor…?'

'Yes,' said Keating reassuringly, 'the local saw-bones, and I'm expecting to have to deliver a baby shortly. So why don't you go through to the dining room and wait in the warm for your mechanic to arrive. There's a couple of friends of mine in there, with my wife, and you can have a bite to eat.'

'*Please* don't open it…' urged the woman.

'It's perfectly all right,' said Keating. 'Now you go in the dining room and I'll be back in two ticks.'

The woman darted into the dining room with Fraser close on her heels, and she slammed the door behind her. Keating chuckled, and opened the front door. Then his eyes widened in surprise.

Shaw stood up instinctively when the woman burst into the dining room. Mrs Shaw and Mrs Keating looked with amazement as she crossed to the French windows and tried to open them. They remained closed.

'What on earth...?' began Mrs Shaw, but then Mrs Keating put a calming hand on the woman's arm. Shaw guessed that she, as her husband's unofficial receptionist, was used to dealing with people in distress.

'The key's gone missing from that door,' said Mrs Keating, smiling benignly at the woman. 'If you want to go outside you'll have to go through the kitchen. Shall I show you?'

'No,' hissed the woman. 'Those men, they'll see me. They mustn't see me!'

Shaw could hear low voices from the front door and noticed the woman was shaking with fright.

'You'll be quite all right in here with us, ma'am,' said Shaw in a low voice. 'With your permission, Mrs Keating, I shall lock the door.'

Mrs Keating gave him a knowing nod and Shaw moved quietly to the door of the dining room, closing it gently and turning the key in the lock. He noticed that the strange woman relaxed slightly, and she accepted Mrs Keating's offer of a chair by the fire. Shaw listened intently at the door and could just about make out a conversation.

`Sorry to trouble you, but I wonder if you could help us.'

It was a nasal, ingratiating voice with a hint of menace behind the politeness.

'The surgery is closed,' said Keating. 'Come back at

nine o'clock tomorrow.'

'We're not here on medical matters,' said the man.
'Well, we hope not.'

'What is it you want then?'

'Have you by any chance had a young lady in here recently?'

'Several. What of it?'

'Might I ask if one of them was about 25 years of age, rather tall and slim, wearing a nurse's hat and coat? Name of Eleanor Harrington.'

'You may ask but I shan't confirm nor deny. This is a doctor's surgery and there's such a thing as patient confidentiality so whether she's been here or not, I wouldn't tell you.'

'I think you're getting a bit confused,' said the man. 'We're not here on medical matters. You see, Miss Harrington is a friend of ours.'

'Oh yes?'

'Yes, that's right, and we were all out for a drive. A jolly, you might say, up to the George Inn. She was in her car and my two associates and myself were in ours, but then we saw her car broken down by the side of the road. We wondered if she'd come here. Especially as this being a doctor's surgery. We're getting rather worried about her.'

'If this Miss Harrington had broken down why didn't she just wait by the car for you to catch up?'

'Ah...well...we thought of that too, and we're concerned she might have injured herself and perhaps got herself into a bit of a muddle and wandered off. She's...well let's say she sometimes has these...attacks, you see. Prone to make things up, you know.'

'Quite frankly my good fellow,' said Keating, 'I don't like the sound of this. If this woman's not in her right mind, we ought to get the police involved. If you'll be kind enough to wait outside I'll telephone for the village constable and we'll see what he has to say about...'

'I wouldn't do that,' interrupted the man sharply, then he continued in a more conciliatory tone. 'We don't want to cause a fuss, do we? I can see you're a busy man so we'll leave you in peace.'

'Just a moment. If I do happen to find this woman, how do I get in touch with you, Mr....?

'Never mind that,' said the man. 'We'll be...in the area...for a while. I expect we'll have her safe and sound long before you do. Good evening'.

Shaw heard the front door close and then the sound of the bolts being rammed home firmly. He unlocked the dining room door and allowed Keating to enter.

'Have...have they gone?' asked the woman.

'For the moment,' said Keating. 'But I have a feeling they'll be back, so before that happens, perhaps you'd be good enough to tell us what this is all about, Miss Eleanor Harrington. *If* that's your name.'

'Yes, it is.' Eleanor paused and looked uncertainly at the assembled company. 'The Honourable Eleanor Lucinda Harrington if you must know.'

'It's all right, you can trust us,' said Keating soothingly. 'Mr Shaw here is the local parson, and this is his wife, and this is *my* wife. You're among friends. Now tell us what's going on.'

'How can I be sure I can trust you...?' said Eleanor.

'If I'd wanted to hand you over to those men I could have done so just now, or I could have telephoned the police,' said Keating. 'I didn't because I could tell something wasn't quite right about the whole thing. You've been kept in restraints, haven't you? And had hypodermic injections, too.'

'How...did you know?'

'Those marks around your wrists and up your arm. I worked in an asylum in Dublin before I went into general practice.'

'I'm not mad!' exclaimed Eleanor forcefully.

'Hush now, did I say you were?' replied Keating. 'I didn't like the look of those fellows. For one thing, they were wearing the same kind of outfits the chaps in the Dublin asylum wore.'

'I told you I'm not mad!' insisted Eleanor.

'And I told you I never said you were,' rejoined Keating. 'How many seats are there in your motor car, Miss Harrington?'

'What...?' asked Eleanor in a confused voice.

'How many seats?'

'Five, I think. Why?'

'There were three of them and one of you. That's four. Why did you need two motor cars just to go for a jolly up to the George?'

'The George...?'

'Miss Harrington,' said Keating kindly, 'the George is a public house up the road, and one you've clearly never heard of. And I don't think those men were your friends like they said, were they? Now, if you want me to help you, you'll have to give me a wee bit of the truth.'

'All right,' sighed Eleanor. 'I'll tell you.'

'Thank you,' replied Keating. 'And have you been

given something to eat?'

'Yes, you've all been very kind,' said Eleanor. 'I'll be as brief as I can. I'm not mad, or anything like that. I can't tell you the full story, I simply can't, but for reasons I can't divulge – so please don't ask me to – I was put into…that place…to be kept out of the way.'

'What place?' asked Keating.

'I don't know what it's called,' said Eleanor with obvious distaste, 'but it's about five miles up the road, set back in some woods. A large house, about a century old or so.'

'Of grey stone construction, surrounded by a high wall?' asked Shaw.

'Yes, that's right,' said Eleanor. 'I don't know the name or address of it, but there were lots of pine trees.'

'That sounds to me like the house known as Ravenswood,' said Shaw. 'It was uninhabited for some years but I believe re-opened as some sort of…nursing home.'

'You mean the old place off the Norwich Road, near Addenham Magna?' asked Mrs Shaw. 'It's not on any of the lists of nursing homes anyone in our Ladies' Guild visits, as far as I know.'

'It wouldn't be,' said Eleanor grimly. 'I don't quite understand *what* the place is, but it's not being used for anything as benificent as nursing. At least two patients have died already in the few months I've been there.'

'And it's not on any official asylum lists that I know of,' added Keating.

'You presumably managed to get away?' said Mrs Keating. 'You must be terribly brave.'

'I wouldn't call it that,' said Eleanor. 'Foolhardy,

perhaps. But yes, I got out. But the car I took...stole, I suppose... had something wrong with it and I crashed into a tree and passed out. It can't have been for more than a minute or so, as by the time I came to, those men were just pulling up nearby. I managed to give them the slip through a little wood and came across this place.'

'But why not tell us that straight away, instead of telephoning for a mechanic?' asked Mrs Shaw.

'If you'd been able to observe Miss Harrington in the hall mirror,' said Keating, 'you'd have seen she had her finger on the telephone cradle the whole time. You didn't make that call, did you?'

'Am I that easy to see through?' asked Eleanor. 'I had to make up some sort of story to be able to spend some time in your house, in the hope those men wouldn't find me. But of course, it was silly of me. I should have known they would come to the house nearest to where I left the car. Look, I'm sorry to have put you all to this trouble. I'll leave you in peace. I have friends who may be able to motor out here to help me. If you will allow me to telephone them.'

She got up to go but Keating put a hand on her shoulder and she sat back down. 'Just wait there a moment, will you?' he asked, and left the room. Soon afterwards he returned.

'Just as I thought,' he said grimly. 'I had a peek through the curtains of the consulting room, and they're out there. The men. Sitting in a car at the end of the lane. I could tell they didn't believe me when I said you'd not been here.'

'I think this has gone far enough,' said Shaw. 'We must telephone for Constable Arbon.'

'No!' Eleanor stood up sharply. 'If the police get involved they'll send me back there. To that place. You can't let them...you can't!'

'Now, now, now,' admonished Keating firmly but calmly. 'Nobody's going anywhere or telephoning anybody just now. You sit here while the vicar and I have a little chat about what we're going to do. Mr Shaw?'

Shaw stood up. Mrs Keating turned to her husband. 'Darling, Miss Harrington looks terribly cold. Why don't I lend her a frock, and some stockings?'

'A good idea,' said Keating. 'You're about the same size.'

'I don't want to impose any more than I already...' began Eleanor.

'Nonsense,' said Mrs Keating, leading her to the door. 'Now you come upstairs and pick out something. Mrs Shaw, you come along too for a second opinion on what looks best. You can post the frock back to me when you're all settled...with your friends.'

Once the ladies had left, Shaw and Keating went into the consulting room at the front of the house. Keating opened the curtains a fraction and looked out.

'Still there,' he said. 'So we need a plan of action. Any thoughts?'

Shaw thought for a moment. 'Miss Harrington claims to have friends who will help her, but what if they are in collusion with her to escape from a place where she is being lawfully held for her own safety? I still think we ought to telephone the police in the first instance. Arbon is a good fellow, and he won't allow these men to take Miss Harrington away with them without observing the correct form in these matters, particularly if you and I insist upon it.'

'Hmm, perhaps you're right,' said Keating. 'There's paperwork and so on that has to be done when a person is committed. But there's something I don't like about this. Now, Miss Harrington *could* be what they call delusional, and she may think that there are men after her when there aren't. That's a common enough form of mental affliction.

'But we know there *are* men after her, and I don't like the look of them. And that girl's been doped, I'm pretty sure of it; I fancy I saw needle marks on her arm. Well, that *might* happen for medical reasons, but why is she half-starved as well?'

'She did indeed seem ravenous when your wife offered her some food,' observed Shaw.

'It's possible she's refused to eat, and has had to be force fed,' mused Keating, 'and you don't get very fat on Bovril poured down your throat through a tube; but there's too many question marks about all this. Now, it's just possible she's addicted to diamorphine, which would explain the weight loss and the needle marks.'

'Diamorphine?' asked Shaw.

'You've probably heard it called heroin,' said Keating. 'It could be, and I'm not saying it is, that she's been kept in a sort of drying-out place for those poor souls. But I've never heard of one using manacles like those marks on her wrists suggest, or sending out a trio of gangsters in search of runaways. Those nursing homes can't legally hold such patients against their will.'

'Very well,' said Shaw. 'I think I have heard enough. If you will allow me, I shall telephone the police house.'

'I have a better idea,' said Keating. 'We'll encourage Miss Harrington to stay the night here and tell her she can go to her friends in the morning. In the meantime I'll telephone the county asylum and arrange for the proper assessments to be made.

'I'm treating her as my patient from now on and if she's declared sane she can go to these friends of hers. If she's not, well then we'll see about this Ravenswood place and make sure they've got the proper credentials to be looking after her before we hand her over. If anything looks wrong, she doesn't go back there.'

'Very well,' said Shaw. 'Perhaps we ought to telephone the county asylum right away. I know the resident chaplain there. If you allow me, I shall speak to him and discuss what is best to do.'

'All right,' said Keating. He opened the door and gestured to the telephone on the table in the hallway, and Shaw picked up the receiver. A puzzled frown crossed his face, and he rattled the cradle several times.

'Hello…hello, operator?' he said, and then handed the receiver to Keating, who listened for a moment then put the instrument down. A cold wave of fear passed momentarily through Shaw's midriff and he looked at Keating.

'That settles it then,' said the doctor. 'If I'm not very much mistaken, those men have cut the telephone line.'

Chapter Two

'We must act quickly,' said Shaw. 'If they have cut the line then they believe Miss Harrington is in here, and they are likely to use force to get her.'

'And that means they're definitely not on the level,' added Keating.

Shaw nodded. 'Are all the doors and windows locked?'

'Yes, Alice always shuts them up at dusk.'

Keating began pacing nervously up and down the room. 'But they won't last long if they really want to get inside. And they could use a battering ram to get in and there's nobody living nearby enough to hear it.'

'I did not see the men at the door,' said Shaw. 'Would you consider them to be physically superior to our combined forces?'

'I'll say they were!' replied Keating with a grim laugh. 'Two of them were built like prop-forwards, and the other looked like the sort of fellow who brings a knife to a fist fight. I might be able to get a knock-out injection into one of them, but not all three at the same time…blast it, if only I had a gun in the house!'

'In my experience, violence is seldom if ever the answer to anything,' replied Shaw. 'There must be another way…'

He bowed his head momentarily and prayed for

guidance quickly and wordlessly, like a sinking ship firing a flare into a storm. Immediately the answer came, like a burst of light amid the darkness. Of course!

Offering up hurried thanks, he turned to Keating.

'You did not mention the presence of myself and my wife to the men, did you?'

Keating replied in the negative.

'Good,' said Shaw. 'They therefore have no idea of how many people are in the house.'

'And…?'

'My dear Keating. Man became lord of the animals not through physical strength but through using his mind. His cunning. We shall do the same. Is your motor car in full working order?'

'Yes of course, but…'

'Would you gather the ladies in the consulting room please? Quickly now.'

A few moments later the group of five were assembled in the consulting room and Shaw cautiously peeked out of the curtain.

'They have moved closer. Miss Harrington, I do not wish to alarm you but I believe those men may be about to attempt to remove you by force.'

Mrs Keating gasped and held a hand to her mouth; the other two women were pictures of calm.

'If you follow my instructions you will all be safe,' said Shaw. 'Will you do exactly as I say?'

All three women nodded. Shaw collected the nurse's stolen hat and coat and handed them to Mrs Keating. 'Would you please put these on, and keep the brim of the hat down low over your eyes.'

Mrs Keating paused and looked at her husband,

whose eyes lit up. 'Shaw you old devil, I think I know what you're up to! Go on my dear, you'll be perfectly all right.'

Mrs Keating put on the hat and coat. 'Now,' said Shaw, 'from a distance you will look much the same as Miss Harrington.'

'But what good will that be if they break in here?' implored Eleanor. 'They won't be fooled by that.'

'Have faith, Miss Harrington,' said Shaw. 'I shall explain.'

A few moments later, Shaw and his wife watched discreetly from the bedroom window with Miss Harrington beside them. Down on the gravel drive below, Keating brought his car around to just outside the porch, and then opened the door.

He kept the hallway light on for a moment, so that anybody watching would see momentarily what was happening, but not so long that it would seem too obvious. He then bundled his wife into the car and sped off.

Eleanor almost shrieked with delight as they saw a large car pass the house in hot pursuit.

'It worked, Mr Shaw, it worked!' she exclaimed. 'Oh, I could *kiss* you!'

Shaw felt himself blush. 'Don't hold back on my account, Miss Harrington,' said Mrs Shaw with a smile. 'It was rather clever, wasn't it? But are you sure they will be all right, Lucian?'

'Keating will drive into the village where there will be people about and he will be within shouting distance of the police house,' said Shaw. 'We need not worry for them. But now, Miss Harrington, we must get you away from here by the back lane. You can stay with us at the vicarage tonight and then in the morning we can get this whole business sorted out.'

'I...very well then,' said Eleanor with a weak smile, but Shaw noticed a look of worry cross her face.

'That's right my dear,' said Keating as he checked the rear view mirror. 'Look around a couple of times as if you're worried we're being followed.'

His wife complied, and Keating saw the large car behind them draw closer.

'Come...into my parlour, said the spider to the nasty flies...' he murmured, and drew the car up alongside a little row of cottages on the edge of Lower Addenham. At the end of the terrace was the Bull, the village's smaller inn. It was a mild night and the door was open; Keating eased the car forward until it was within sight of the door.

The large car that had been following them pulled up behind them. There was a tap on the passenger window and Mrs Keating slid it open.

'Now that was a waste of everybody's time, wasn't it, Miss Harrington,' said the nasal-voiced man. 'Come along now, let's get you home.'

Mrs Keating turned to face him and the larger man with him, removing her hat as she did so. 'I think you must be mistaken. My name isn't Harrington. May I be of any assistance?' She smiled sweetly.

'I *told* you they'd try something like...' yelled the

smaller of the two men at his companion, and then lowered his voice as his eyes flicked to the row of terraces beyond the car.

Keating looked to his right to see a large, heavily built man emerge from one of the cottages, holding an open shotgun and a cleaning rag.

'Everything all roite, doctor?' he asked, eyeing the men with suspicion.

'Quite all right thank you, Mr Jepson,' said Keating jovially. 'These gentlemen were just asking the way to the police station. I won't keep your wife much longer.'

'You'll be hearing from us,' snapped the nasal-voiced man, who spat on the ground in front of the car and then hurried back to his own vehicle, with the larger man lumbering behind.

Mrs Keating exhaled sharply. 'Thank God that worked.'

'You did marvellously my dear,' said Keating. 'Now you come inside with me and you can chat to Mrs Jepson about all the baby clothes she's knitting. Why, what's the matter now? They've gone, and the Shaws will be away with Miss Harrington to safety long since.'

'Paddy,' she said, looking with a worried expression in the direction that the car had just gone, 'didn't you say there were *three* men at the door when they called?'

'I did. Two big ones and the little one.'

'There were only two men in that car.'

A worried frown crossed Keating's face as he opened the car door.

'Curse me for an idiot, I saw the three of them myself at my own front door, and I clean forgot in the excitement. Wait here while I tell Jepson we can't stay.

The midwife will have to cope on her own. We'd better get back home as soon as we can. I've a nasty feeling we haven't been as clever as we'd like to think.'

'Come along, Miss Harrington,' said Shaw, once the sound of the vehicles had died away. 'It will not be long before our little deception is found out, and those men are likely to return when that happens. It is not far to the vicarage through the back lane, and then you can rest quietly there until the morning.'

Shaw led the way down the stairs into the hallway, but then Eleanor paused.

'I know it sounds silly,' she said, 'but I feel I must look an awful fright. I don't suppose you have little bit of powder and lipstick, Mrs Shaw?'

'My dear lady, there really isn't time to…' began Shaw, but he was cut off by his wife.

'Of course, Miss Harrington,' she said brightly. 'We women know how important it is to look our best in difficult circumstances. Take my handbag, dear. You'll find everything in there, and the little cloakroom I believe is just across there, by the stairs. But *do* be quick – we must leave as soon as possible.'

A few moments later Shaw looked nervously through the front and back windows, and then tapped on the door of the cloakroom. 'Do hurry please, Miss Harrington,' he said. The only sound he could hear was that of running water from the tap. Nervously he glanced at his watch. A minute passed, and he banged on the door loudly.

'Miss Harrington,' he said firmly. 'Open this door immediately.'

'Are you all right, dear?' enquired Mrs Shaw. 'Ought you to break it down, Lucian?' she asked.

'I shan't waste my energy,' sighed Shaw. 'I think I know what's happened. Come outside with me.'

They went out through the kitchen door and round to the back of the house. Fraser followed them and began yelping, until Shaw ordered him to be quiet.

They stood and looked at the little bathroom window; the sash had been pulled up. They looked inside and the room was empty.

'We'll have to go after her,' said Mrs Shaw plaintively. 'We can't just leave her.'

'We can't just go running off into the woods at night either,' said Shaw. 'There's no point going after her until Keating comes back with his motor car. She could have gone in any direction, wild with panic. We've told her she's welcome at the vicarage so if she wants us to help her she'll go there.'

Mrs Shaw reached through the window to retrieve an object. 'At least she left my handbag,' she said, looking down into the open reticule. 'But...oh...she's taken my purse. There were 35 shillings in there, for Hettie's wages...'

'She left you a message, as well,' said Shaw, pointing to the mirror. In large letters, written with lipstick, appeared the message: I AM SORRY. I WILL PAY YOU BACK.

Fraser began snarling again, and they stood still. For a moment Shaw thought he heard movement beyond the hedge, where a little path ran down through the woods, but then it was drowned out by the noise of a motor car pulling up to the house. Shaw kept close to the wall and looked round the front of the building, then sighed with relief as he saw it was Dr and Mrs Keating.

'Is she all right?' exclaimed Keating as he got out of the car. 'We think they kept one of the men here, watching the place while the other two followed us.'

'She's gone,' said Shaw. 'She got through the bathroom window some minutes ago, taking my wife's purse with her.'

'Blast it all,' said Keating. 'Why the devil did she have to do that? Now she's likely got a man following her and we've no idea where she's got to.'

'I think we have no choice but to involve the police,' said Shaw.

'You're right,' replied Keating. 'I'll telephone them and...Lord's sake, they cut the lines, didn't they. Come along, we'll drive straight to the police house, and keep an eye out for Miss Harrington along the way.'

Chief Inspector George Ludd of Midchester Police sighed as he looked around the back room of the little police house at Lower Addenham. A heavy-set man with greying hair and a moustache which drooped more with each passing year, he wore the plain-clothes policeman's uniform of tightly belted mackintosh and trilby hat, which he kept on despite the warm fug emanating from the little coal fire in the corner of the room.

He looked intently at Reverend Shaw, Mrs Shaw and the Keatings, who sat before him on upright wooden chairs.

'This village,' he said wearily, 'seems to attract trouble like a jam pot attracts flies. And whenever the flies are round the pot, you never seem far away either, Mr Shaw.'

'I suppose I should be flattered that you consider me to be neither the jam pot nor one of the flies,' said Shaw.

'You can hardly blame the vicar,' said Keating. 'It was only by chance he was having supper with us when Miss Harrington turned up.'

'Ye-s,' said Ludd slowly, 'but it was he who got PC Arbon to telephone for me and have me give up my horticultural society meeting to come out here to the middle of nowhere. It sounds like a perfectly straightforward case of a lunatic escaping from an asylum, so I don't see why I should be involved.'

'My dear Chief Inspector,' said Shaw, 'you could have quite easily delegated the case to PC Arbon, but come you did. I rather think you wanted a reason to get away from your horticultural meeting.'

Ludd gave out something between a laugh and a grunt. 'Well, they do go on, some of those fellows. There's only so much one can learn about the uses of manure, which when you think about it, is quite literally a pile of old…ah, ahem.'

'It's all very well to exchange pleasantries,' said Mrs Keating, 'but what are we going to do about poor Miss Harrington?'

'Mrs Keating,' sighed Ludd, 'I think we've done about

all we can do. We've had Arbon and the two special constables from the village combing the area on bicycles, plus we've drafted in men from Addenham Magna and Great Netley. There's been no sign of her or these three men who you say were threatening her.'

'We don't just *say* they were threatening her,' said Keating angrily, 'they *were* threatening her.'

'All right, doctor, all right,' said Ludd. 'But I drove all along that road and I didn't see any sign of a car smash, so that part of Miss Harrington's story doesn't fit. I even rang the bell at the gate of this Ravenswood place, but it was all dark and shut-up and nobody answered. Without a search warrant there's not much more I can do.'

'Well that's convenient,' said Keating angrily. 'Now I've a mind to get in my car and drive up that road myself and find out what the devil is going on there, and…'

He was interrupted by the shrill sound of an electric bell. Ludd picked up the candlestick telephone and held it to his ear.

'Ludd speaking…yes…yes…I see. And after that? I see. All right, well done. Yes, stand them down. I'll get on to the Metropolitan Police about it. Yes, cheer-oh.'

'Well?' said Keating.

'A woman of Miss Harrington's description was seen getting on the branch line at Lower Addenham station. The constable telephoned through to Great Netley to have her picked up, but she gave them the slip. They think she might have changed to another train, probably going to London as that was the last one stopping there. There's not much more we can do now.

I'll put out a missing person's description but unless she's considered dangerous there won't be much done about it.'

'Oh dear,' said Mrs Keating.

'At least those men didn't get to her,' said Mrs Shaw. 'Hopefully with that money she'll be able to get to those friends she mentioned.'

'Money?' asked Ludd. 'How did she have money if she'd just escaped from a loony bin?'

'Oh it was, a…a loan,' said Mrs Shaw with some embarrassment. 'She didn't steal it or anything like that. I…enabled…her to borrow some money. 35 shillings.'

Ludd sighed. 'I must say you all seem to have been uncommonly generous to this person. It would have been much easier for all concerned if you'd let those orderlies take her back to where she was supposed to be.'

'You didn't see them,' said Keating. 'They were thugs. I wouldn't have put a heavyweight boxer into their charge. And Miss Harrington claimed she was kept there under false pretences.'

'Well, if she's a loony she would say that, wouldn't she?,' asked Ludd with some impatience.

Keating bridled. 'I daresay I've had a little more experience than you in these matters and I'm not entirely sure she was a "loony" as you put it. Now, if you're not going to speak to those people at Ravenswood, then I will.'

'Perhaps, Dr Keating, that would not be a good idea,' said Shaw. 'After all, they have seen you. But they have not seen me. I could make a pastoral visit. After all, it is just on the edge of the parish, and…'

'*Oh* no!' said Ludd firmly, pushing his hat brim up in exasperation. 'I'm not having you playing detective and making a whole lot of mess for me to clean up, Mr Shaw. I will go there myself tomorrow morning, and find out just what sort of place it is, and if there's anything untoward going on, we'll get the proper authorities to deal with it. The Board of Guardians or whatever they are called now. But for now as it's nearly eleven o'clock I suggest we all go home!'

Eleanor awoke with a start, momentarily unsure of where she was. Then it came back to her; she was in a compartment on a London-bound train. She had managed to get the last train out of the little station at Lower Addenham and then changed at Great Netley for the express.

For a moment she thought she had been followed. She had noticed a heavily built man in the shadows at the end of the platform at Great Netley, but it was probably just her imagination, she decided. She carefully selected a compartment that had other people in it, and although she tried to stay awake, before the train had reached Colchester she was fast asleep.

She checked the pocket of her frock to reassure herself that the purse she had taken from Mrs Shaw's handbag was still in her possession, then looked at her fellow passengers opposite.

An elderly, kindly looking lady, a fat man, perhaps a commercial traveller, asleep with his mouth open, and a youth in spectacles absorbed in a book. She occasionally glanced nervously at the corridor when anyone walked past, but nobody seemed to take an interest in her.

She raised her left wrist and then sighed as she remembered she had no watch. The old lady opposite must have read her mind, as she looked at her own tiny timepiece.

'Nearly eleven o'clock,' she said brightly. 'We shall be in London quite soon.'

'Thank you,' said Eleanor distractedly, as she looked at endless rows of gaslit streets which passed the window, their ranks broken occasionally by brightly lit cinemas and motor garages. At last! Finally she could lose herself, anonymous among the teeming millions of the capital, and, if she could find her friends, she would have time to work out what to do.

Eventually they reached the terminus at Liverpool Street, and Eleanor hurried down into the Underground. It was quiet at first, the only other person a uniformed man with a broom slowly sweeping up, and she looked round nervously at the long empty platform, fancying she saw a movement in the shadows by the exit.

Then the station was filled with noise as a crowd began to pour down the staircase. She guessed a theatre or music hall had just turned out, as some of the people were in evening dress and holding programmes, all chattering brightly to each other. Then she looked up and saw him.

She was right – she *had* been followed. All the way from Suffolk! Cold fear welled up in her stomach and she swallowed hard, forcing herself to remain calm. It was the orderly, Barton. He had a cap pulled down over his eyes and his overcoat collar turned up, but she would have recognised his lumbering walk and ape-like hands anywhere.

He began walking towards her. The sound of a train approaching grew louder, but she dared not wait for it, even though logically it was unlikely Barton would try anything with so many people around. But she was no longer thinking logically.

She realised she was cut off from the exit by the theatre crowd, and she attempted to make her way through the dense mass of people as quickly as she could. She was too distracted to apologise, and this oversight provoked the restrained indignity of an English crowd which notices someone is not playing by the rules. There were mutterings of 'manners!' '*Do* you mind!' and in coarser tones, ''ere, wait your blooming turn!'

She looked round to see Barton only a few feet away, a bland, expressionless look on his face, but she could see him flexing the thick fingers on his enormous hands. Those hands! The thought of them touching her as they had done on so many occasions filled her with revulsion.

The laughing, braying crowd, with its glowing, drink-reddened faces, pressed ever closer to her and seemed to move like a herd of animals towards the edge of the platform. 'Ere!' came a tipsy shout. 'Watch out there, you'll have us all over the blinking edge!'

A woman laughed hysterically and then was drowned out by the roar of the train as it neared the mouth of the tunnel. The last thing Eleanor ever felt was the irresistible force of Barton's hands as they pushed her over the edge of the platform.

The following morning dawned bright and clear, the March sunshine beaming through the still-bare trees, giving a foretaste of the spring that would soon come. Chief Inspector Ludd was in a bouyant mood as he drove his gleaming Austin motor car along the long, straight road which led from Lower Addenham to Addenham Magna. The previous night he had been unable to see much along the way, but now he slowed down as he saw a long mark along the mud by the side of the road.

He parked his car carefully on the verge and crossed to the other side. There was the clear tyre track in the mud, which stretched for some fifty yards or so until it veered off into the woodland by the road. He walked its length, and noticed that three tyre tracks and a deep gouged line became visible in the mulch, leading up to a silver birch tree.

The tree had a large cut on one side, as if it had been hit with a blunt axe; he saw something glint in the leaves around its base, and bent down to pick up a few slivers of glass and some flakes of green paint which crumbled at his touch. He took out a brown envelope from his pocket and carefully placed the fragments of glass and paint into it.

'She hit the tree here,' he muttered to himself, dimly aware that he seemed to be talking to himself a lot more nowadays, especially if he was working alone. 'But what's this line where the other tyre mark should be?,' he continued. 'Of course! The wheel came off and she lost control…and the other tyre marks are wider…some sort of recovery truck must have removed the car.'

He smiled in satisfaction, and returned to his car. A few minutes later he pulled up at a pair of large wrought-iron gates in a high, moss-covered brick wall. He noticed that the wall had a line of broken glass set along its apex, and that the black paint of the gates was freshly chipped and scored.

The night before the house had appeared nothing but a silhouette, but now he shuddered slightly as he looked at it. The building was grey and stained, with moss covered parapets and gables, the large plate glass windows fronted with metal bars. Even the bright sunshine did not seem able to dispel the atmosphere of damp despair which emanated from it.

He rang the old-fashioned bell-pull at the gate, and a heavily built man with close-cropped hair shuffled out of the little gatehouse. He was dressed in a semi-official cap and tunic, like a park-keeper or the commissionaire of a run-down cinema, except that he had a large bunch of keys on a chain at his belt, like a gaoler.

'Yus?' enquired the man. 'Callers is by appointment only.'

'I don't need an appointment, matey,' said Ludd brightly. 'I'm a policeman.' He showed his warrant card to the man, who squinted at it suspiciously through the gate. 'Tell whoever's in charge of this place I'd like to speak to him. Right away, there's a good fellow.'

The man shrugged and went into the gatehouse, where Ludd saw him wind up an old-fashioned crank-telephone. After a brief conversation, he returned to the gate.

'Someone'll be down presently.'

'If you'll open this gate I'll walk up there myself and save him the trouble.'

'Be down presently.'

The man disappeared into the gatehouse. Ludd tapped his foot impatiently and considered lighting a cigarette, then dismissed the idea as he saw a figure approach him.

A tall man in early middle age, with swept back hair and a patrician bearing, wearing a doctor's white coat over a well tailored suit, looked blandly at Ludd through the railings.

'How can I help you, ah, Inspector, Legg, was it?'

'Chief Inspector Ludd. And your name sir?'

'Doctor Julian Landis. I'm in charge of this establishment.'

'May we talk inside, sir?'

'I'm sorry Chief Inspector, but no. We have to maintain very strict security here, due to the nature of the work we do. Unless you have written permission from the county medical authorities, I regret...'

Landis waived his hand airily as if the matter were entirely out of his control.

Ludd smiled politely. 'I understand, sir. It's just that we've had reports of a motor accident down the road and I wondered if you knew anything about it. We're looking for witnesses.'

'Do they send Chief Inspectors to look into that sort of thing?' asked Landis in a puzzled tone.

'Not usually, sir,' replied Ludd, 'but I happened to be

free this morning. By the way, have you lost any of your inmates lately?'

Landis chuckled. 'Inmates? This is a private nursing home, Chief Inspector. We prefer to call them residents.'

'All right then, have you lost any residents lately?'

'Everyone is accounted for, thank you. Should I be concerned about anyone in particular? I'm not quite sure what you're suggesting.'

'If somebody wanted to leave,' said Ludd carefully, 'for example, a person who wasn't happy with the treatment he...or she...was receiving in your care, how would that person go about it?'

'My good man,' said Landis, 'I don't think you can expect me to divulge details like that. Am I being accused of something?'

This could go on all day, thought Ludd. He recognised evasion when he saw it, but without any firm evidence of wrong-doing there was little he could achieve at this stage, and he did not wish to overplay his hand. He smiled and touched the brim of his hat.

'Of course not, sir,' he said cheerily. 'I'm sorry to have disturbed you. If you do remember anything about that car you said hit that tree down the road, you'll be sure to let the police know, won't you?'

'I didn't say anything about a car hitting a tree, Chief Inspector,' said Landis with a patient smile. 'You brought up the subject. But if I do hear anything I shall most certainly seek you out. Good day.'

'Good day, sir,' said Ludd, and then looked more closely at the chipped and warped gate in front of him. He noticed some small flecks of green paint embedded in the black metal. 'My word,' he exclaimed. 'Looks like a rhinoceros had a go at that. You're not keeping wild animals in there, are you, doctor?' he added with a chuckle.

Landis merely gave a brittle smile. 'Good day,' he repeated, and strode off towards the house without looking back.

Ludd deftly picked a small flake of green paint from the gate and kept it under his fingernail until he returned to his car, where he placed it carefully in another envelope. He then drove rapidly back to Midchester and began to make a series of telephone calls.

Chapter Three

Shaw sat in the little study of Lower Addenham's vicarage, working on his sermon for the following Sunday. His text was the eighth verse of the third chapter of the Epistle to the Romans, in which St Paul warns against doing evil in the hope that good may come of it.

It was a difficult topic and he wished now that he had not started on it. He puffed on his pipe thoughtfully, hoping for inspiration, but none came.

He decided it was hopeless, and that he would look at the other appointed lessons for the forthcoming Sunday to see if they might prove easier to write about. He rubbed his eyes wearily. Had the excitements of the previous night not occurred he might have had the energy to tackle it, but now he could not stop thinking about what might have happened to Eleanor Harrington.

There was a knock at the door; he opened it and saw his wife in the doorway. He realised immediately that something was wrong.

'Yes my dear? Has there been some news?' he asked, noticing she was holding the morning paper which he had not yet had a chance to read.

She placed it wordlessly on his desk and pointed to an article on the 'stop press' section of the back page.

WOMAN KILLED BY TRAIN

An unidentified woman approximately 25 years of age was killed after falling into the path of an oncoming train from the westbound District Railway platform at London's Liverpool Street station around 11pm last night. She was in possession of a purse which police believe may be stolen. Anyone who witnessed the incident should inform London Transport Police c/o Liverpool Street Station.

'It's her, isn't it?' said Mrs Shaw. 'Miss Harrington. It *must* be.'

Shaw sighed and pushed the newspaper away. 'We cannot be sure…'

'No, it must be her,' said Mrs Shaw sadly. 'Trains coming in from Suffolk terminate at Liverpool Street. And she had my purse. That's why the police said it was stolen.'

'But Marion, dear,' said Shaw slowly, 'even if it were your purse, why would they assume it was stolen rather than that it belonged to the dead girl?'

'You're not the only amateur detective in this house,' said Mrs Shaw. 'My name and address are on a label sewn into the lining of the purse. But I also, for reasons that I admit are largely vanity, have for some months been carrying around in it that little cutting from the local newspaper about me winning the prize for the harvest festival flower display.'

'I see,' said Shaw. 'The cutting, I recall, showed a rather good photograph of you, together with your name. The police presumably saw this and deduced that Miss Harrington…if it *was* her, was not the owner of the purse and that therefore she may have stolen it. But all this is conjecture.'

'I think you should telephone Chief Inspector Ludd,' said Mrs Shaw. 'If it *was* my purse, he's bound to come calling sooner or later…'

She was cut off by the jangling sound of the front door bell.

'If that is Chief Inspector Ludd,' said Shaw, rising from his seat, 'then the British police are far more efficient than I could ever have imagined.'

There was a knock on the study door and Hettie, the maid-of-all-work, entered the room.

'Beg pardon, sir, mum, there's someone at the door.'

'Yes, thank you Hettie,' said Shaw. 'Show the Chief Inspector in, please.'

A look of confusion crossed the servant's face. 'Oh it's not *'im*, sir. It's the doctor – Doctor Keating.'

Keating was shown into the study and after passing the time of day quickly with Shaw and his wife, he pointed to the newspaper on the desk.

'You've seen it too, then? Think it's her?'

'We cannot be certain,' said Shaw. 'I have no doubt Chief Inspector Ludd will be able to tell us.'

'Let's hope so,' said Keating. 'But in the meantime, I've been doing a bit of investigating myself by telephone. I've been feeding pennies into the call-box all morning, as the GPO says it'll be days before they mend my telephone. They were most suspicious about it, and I had to pretend it was me cut it myself while trimming the hedge. Anyway, I've been on to the county asylum and a couple of other doctors I know in the district, asking about that Ravenswood place.'

'And…?' asked Shaw, as he refilled his pipe.

'And it's all a bit shady,' said Keating. 'The upshot is, it doesn't seem to be on any official list of private asylums or have gone through any of the vetting procedures required to set up such a place. My pal in the county asylum says his governor didn't seem to want to discuss it. In short, it's not just a stone wall around the place, there's a wall of silence, too.'

Chief Inspector Ludd leaned forward over his desk in his office at Midchester Police headquarters, and excitedly opened the buff envelope which had just been placed into his hands by a motorcycle despatch rider. He looked at the large, glossy photograph that was contained in it, and frowned.

Then the telephone rang. He picked it up, and was informed by the operator that his London call was ready.

'Hello, Inspector Riley?' he asked. 'This is Chief Inspector Ludd, Midchester C.I.D. We spoke earlier.'

Ludd had seen the newspaper article about the woman killed by a train earlier that day, and had immediately telephoned Trunks and asked to be put through to Liverpool Street Station's police.

After some effort he managed to speak to the detective in charge, who had listened patiently as Shaw had explained the reasons for his second call. He couldn't help thinking the man sounded less enthusiastic this time, but he ploughed ahead, conscious of the cost of a long call to London.

'I've got the photograph of the dead girl,' he said rapidly. 'Well done for getting that here on the train so fast, and I arranged for a despatch rider to pick it up from the station too. So the trail's still hot. And here's another thing. I've compared those flecks of green paint I mentioned before, and I think they're from the same vehicle. I can't be sure of course until I get the experts to have a look, but in the meantime I'm fairly sure that proves somebody broke out of that Ravenswood place. Now, if it was that girl that went under the train, we...'

He stopped, realising he had been gassing on for far too long. 'Are you still there, Riley?' he asked.

Riley was indeed still there, and spoke briefly and succinctly to Ludd. A deep frown began to spread across the Chief Inspector's face.

'He definitely said that? The Chief Constable? Then why did you send me the photogr...I see, you hadn't been told then. An accident? But...well, I must say I don't like the sound of...yes I know orders are orders, but...hello?'

There was a dry click as Riley hung up.

'Charming,' he grunted, and then the telephone rang again. This time, it was the Chief Constable of Suffolk.

Ludd instinctively stood up and straightened his tie, and listened to his superior officer speaking.

'Yes sir, I've just been speaking to them long-distance. Yes, they told me the same thing. May I ask who...but...I see. No, I'm not questioning your authority, sir. And yes...I know, orders are orders. Goodbye, sir.'

'It stinks, Mr Shaw. That's all I can say, it stinks, like a three day old haddock in a heatwave,' said Chief Inspector Ludd as he paced angrily up and down the threadbare persian carpet in front of the fireplace in Shaw's study.

'More tea, Chief Inspector?' said Shaw, offering to fill up the detective's cup and noticing it had barely been touched. 'Or perhaps a cigarette? These Turkish ones are very soothing.' He extended the box of cigarettes to Ludd, but it was waved away. On all the occasions he had met him, Shaw could not recall the man looking so agitated.

'You have definitely been relieved of *all* duties regarding Miss Harrington's case?' asked Shaw.

'It's not just me they've pulled, Mr Shaw, it's *everybody*. The London Transport police have been told not to pursue the matter as well. A simple accident, and that's that.'

'Told, by whom?' enquired Shaw.

'That's just it,' said Ludd. 'Nobody will tell me. The London Transport man, Riley, said it was my Chief Constable that told them to close it down, but my Chief Constable said it was the London Transport Police that told *him*!'

'I see,' said Shaw. He looked down at the photograph that Ludd had showed him. Eleanor Harrington looked almost peaceful, and had he not known it had been taken by a police pathologist, he might have assumed she was merely sleeping rather than dead. He sighed and handed the photograph back to Ludd.

'And by rights I shouldn't even be showing you that,' said Ludd, 'but I had to know if that girl found dead in London was the one you helped last night. And it *was* her, and that means she may well have been pushed under that train by the same chaps that were following her last night. *And* I told you about those paint marks I found.

'That fellow Landis who runs the place was hiding something, I'm sure of it. It's my belief this Miss Harrington stole a car at Ravenswood and drove it at speed through those gates, then crashed into a tree further down the road. Somebody recovered that vehicle, and if I was to ask around the local garages, I'd find out who. And then…oh, it's no use.'

Ludd slumped back into the armchair by the fire and drained the last of his tea, dropping the cup heavily back into the saucer.

'If there's one thing I don't like,' he said, becoming more calm, 'it's being told not to poke my nose into something. I don't mind it from the criminal fraternity, that's to be expected, but when it's my own superiors…that smarts. And what you told me about Dr Keating finding out that Ravenswood doesn't seem to be entirely legitimate just makes it all the more suspicious.'

'Is there *anything* that can be done?' asked Shaw.

'It's more than my job's worth to pursue this matter now, Mr Shaw,' said Ludd. 'The official shutters have come down. I saw that before when you…' his voice trailed away.

'Yes, Chief Inspector?'

'I saw that before in that business with King Basil'.*

'You mean the assassination?'

'Yes. And the official shutters came down then as well. But I didn't mind that so much because I knew that Special Branch – or whoever it was that took over from me – were doing it for the right reasons, to throw light on it rather than cover it up. And I know you can't talk about that so I won't ask you to. But perhaps…'

'Perhaps you think I may be able to raise the official shutters sufficiently to squeeze through?' asked Shaw, with a raised eyebrow.

'This is a turnup, all right,' said Ludd with a chuckle. 'In the past it's been me in charge of a case and you pestering me about it. Now it could be the other way round.'

'I offered yesterday to visit Ravenswood,' said Shaw. 'Is that the sort of thing you had in mind?'

'Yes…' said Ludd slowly, 'but I'd rather you didn't act alone. I'll wager you know some people that we're not supposed to know about who might be able to help. I've heard mention that you were involved with some very shady characters when the Dean of Midchester was murdered**, for example.'

'My dear Chief Inspector,' said Shaw brightly, 'I neither confirm nor deny such rumours. But I should like to help, and if the official channels are closed, perhaps I may indeed be able to get round them somehow. But I warn you – they may just as easily be blocked at the higher level as they have been at the lower.'

---

*See The King is Dead. **See Murder at Evensong.

'You're right of course,' said Ludd, 'but I'll take that chance. You're a good man, Shaw. I'd like to get to the bottom of all this.'

'So would I, Chief Inspector,' said Shaw. 'May I take these?' he gestured to the envelopes containing the paint slivers and the photograph of Eleanor. 'To show to…ah, that is, for reference.'

'Be my guest,' said Ludd, handing over the envelopes. 'And keep me informed – discreetly.'

'Very well, Chief Inspector. Give me a few days.'

After Ludd had left, Shaw took a small card from his wallet, picked up the telephone and asked the operator for the number on the card. It was a number not listed in any public directory, and when the operator connected him, he asked to speak to a person whom he knew did not exist.

The following day was Wednesday, and Shaw had only one commitment after morning prayer, which was to meet with the Mother's Union. He sent his apologies, and began putting on his raincoat in the little hallway of the vicarage. Fraser, hoping for a walk, trotted back excitedly until Shaw ordered him back to his basket, and he slunk away with a dejected air.

Mrs Shaw appeared at the kitchen doorway. 'You're getting yourself involved again, aren't you?' she said.

'My dear, why…'

'Please don't try to deny it. I heard you speaking to someone on the telephone yesterday in a most furtive manner. You're not *just* going to London to look for antiquarian books, are you?'

'That is part of my reason for travelling, yes, but as for any other matter, I have no idea if I shall be "involved" in anything. I told you that the police appear uninterested in poor Miss Harrington's death, but I may be able to make certain enquiries myself.'

'That's exactly what I said,' replied Mrs Shaw tersely. 'You *are* getting involved.'

'At present all I am doing is conducting a meeting with somebody who may be able to help.'

'Couldn't he – I assume it *is* a he – do that over the telephone?'

'My dear, Maj…ah, that is, the gentleman in question, does not consider the telephone, nor the post, to be an entirely safe form of communication. Instead, we are to meet in person. I really must go now or I shall miss the train.'

'Very well. Here.' She gave a wax-paper parcel to Shaw. 'Hettie has made some sandwiches for your journey.'

'Please thank her for me,' said Shaw. 'And please, do not worry. I shall be back this evening.'

'Oh Lucian do be *careful*,' implored his wife as he closed the door and stepped out into the bright morning.

Major Arthur Wheatley, MM, DSO and Bar, sat at his desk behind a frosted-glass door in an office deep within the bowels of an anonymous building in Whitehall. A heavy-set man with a ruddy complexion and a thick rectangular moustache, he frowned as he heard the chimes of Big Ben in the distance, and looked up at the electric clock hanging over the chimneypiece.

Only eleven! At least the tea trolley would be round soon, he thought, so that was something to look forward to. Then his face brightened as he remembered he had a luncheon appointment with Reverend Shaw. He hadn't let the man explain completely what it was about, of course, but he knew Shaw would only use that telephone number if it was important.

Following his first encounter with Shaw the previous year, Wheatley had hoped that the man might prove useful again at some point; in fact, he had made an official recommendation to that effect, but he had not expected to hear from him so soon.

He looked down at the pile of paperwork on his desk. Blast it all, he thought. It was all the most tedious lot of rubbish. Reports by his underlings of the activities of trade union agitators, German schoolmasters, Russian ballet dancers (he had initially been intrigued by that case until he found out the dancer in question was a man). Reams of nonsense that all had to be gone through.

'At one-thirty pm subject entered public library in Wandsworth High Street and borrowed volume of poetry by DH Lawrence,' he read aloud from one report. 'Should this be investigated further?' He scowled; how he longed for an interesting case!

Of course, he thought, as he shook loose a Woodbine from a crumpled packet, it had been different in the war.

There had been no shortage of adventure then. His mind drifted back to how it had all started.

His first job had been as a Post Office clerk, and so in 1914 he had enlisted in the Royal Engineers Postal Section, and enjoyed, at first, what they called a 'good war'. A capable administrator, he was promoted to sergeant but was largely spared from front line combat due to his trade. But then all that changed in 1917.

He, with a couple of privates, had been laying telephone cable about half a mile behind one of the front line trenches at Ypres. All of a sudden, there was an explosion louder than anything he had heard before; it was not even really a *noise*, because his ears were too damaged to hear it; it was a sort of almighty deafening silence which drowned out the sound of everything, even the distant artillery and chatter of machine-gun fire.

He learned later, when it had been captured by the Canadians, that the noise was from a giant experimental German railway gun, so large that it took two hours to load. It had fired a single shell from six miles away, but one shell had been enough.

Their ears ringing, the three deafened men cautiously made their way to the trench, communicating by sign language. What they saw was hard to believe, and Wheatley blinked as if his eyes as well as his ears were damaged.

Every single man was dead; men he had known and worked with, some of them for three years. The lines of corpses stretched for half a mile in each direction; the officers in the dugouts, and the cooks and orderlies, even the Padre, all lying as if they were sleeping, their bodies seemingly unharmed. The shell had not hit the trench itself but landed some distance away in No Man's Land. The shock wave and subsequent vacuum, however, had been sufficiently powerful to instantly kill every man in the company. Knocked their brains against the insides of their skulls, he was later told; he was reassured they would have felt nothing but that seemed little consolation, the sort of rot that commanding officers wrote in letters home to make grieving widows feel better.

Then Wheatley heard a buzzing noise and realised his hearing was coming back. He looked up to see a speck in the air and as it came closer, he saw that it was a German spotter plane. He found out later they had come to check if the gun required any alterations to its range, but Wheatley could think only that they had come to gloat.

The two privates took cover in a dugout as the plane made a low pass, and Wheatley let them be. He gently eased aside the corpses of the men next to a Lewis gun, and, when the plane made another pass, he calmly fixed it through the weapon's circular sight and pulled the trigger, emptying the entire magazine into the underside of the passing plane.

Flame and black smoke instantly engulfed the flimsy aircraft and it dropped to the ground like a child's kite. There was a ragged cheer from the two men watching from the dugout, but Wheatley wasn't satisfied. He could see a figure moving in the flames.

Heedless of his own safety, Wheatley climbed the trench ladder and walked forward to the stricken craft across No Man's Land. The airman's overalls were on fire, and he staggered forward from the plane holding out his arms imploringly, screaming something in German that Wheatley could not understand.

Wheatley began to take off his greatcoat, then paused.

'Smother him, sarge, or the poor basket's had it!' came a shout from one of the privates.

But Wheatley didn't seem to hear. He put his coat back on and carefully rebuttoned it, then calmly lit a cigarette and watched the man burn to death.

If you had asked him why he had done it, he could not have told you, but something had changed deep within Wheatley. He had begun to hate. And it was not the hot hate of momentary anger; it was cold and calculated and premeditated. He had become a man without mercy.

Then, a blur of action; a staff officer arrived on a horse – a horse, in 1917! He had witnessed the incident as he led a rescue party to the trench. The German gun was captured, and Wheatley was informed that had he not shot down that plane, the pilot would have reported the shortfall in the range, and the giant gun would have destroyed the entire forward line and Brigade headquarters into the bargain.

After that, there had been the Military Medal and then a battlefield commission, and Captain Wheatley had spent the last year of the war volunteering for any and every dangerous job that came his way. He was known as being a 'good man in a scrap' and, as the war ended, he was involved in some clandestine activity which earned him the Distinguished Service Order and, after the Armistice, a promotion to major and a place in the government department in which he now worked.

'I said, come back dear.' Wheatley was jerked back into the present by the dulcet tones of the tea lady.

"Aven't you got nothing better to do than stare into space, Major?' added the woman with a throaty laugh. She and the other servants in the building liked Wheatley's down to earth manner and lack of 'side', as they called it.

'Sorry m'dear,' said Wheatley. 'I was lost in thought.'

'Oh is *that* what they calls sleeping on the job these days,' said the tea lady with a chuckle. 'Ere,' she added, plonking a plate on to his desk, 'you can 'ave an extra biscuit for some energy. Not 'cos you need fattening up, 'cos you don't.'

'Cheek!' exclaimed Wheatley, but he eagerly snatched up the biscuits then slurped the hot tea carefully through his moustache.

After arriving in London, Shaw had browsed for a short while in the second hand bookshops in the Charing Cross Road, picking out a handsomely bound edition of Marcus Aurelius' *Meditations*. Aurelius was one of the 'Virtuous Pagans' who although not a Christian, nevertheless held ideas which tallied in many ways with those of the early Church. He justified the expense (two shillings) by telling himself that it might help with his sermon on not doing evil so that good may come of it, should he re-attempt it, although he was not quite sure *how* it would help.

Realising it was nearly one o'clock, Shaw hurried

down past Trafalgar Square and entered a public house of a somewhat lower social status than he had been expecting. After enquiring at the bar, he was shown upstairs to a small private dining room, in which sat a man in a pinstriped suit with a mug of beer in front of him. The man looked up and wiped a line of froth from his moustache. Shaw saw with relief that he used his left hand for this accomplishment, and then offered his other for Shaw to shake.

'Good to see you, Mr Shaw,' said Wheatley. 'Sit down, sit down. How's the preaching lark? Good I hope. I've taken the liberty of ordering chops and two veg. for you, as that's all they've got on.'

'Thank you, Major Wheatley,' said Shaw as he sat down. 'That will be most welcome. And the "preaching lark" is as rewarding as always. I trust you are well?'

Wheatley chuckled. 'I won't bore you with all my problems so I'll just say yes thank you. I suppose you were expecting something a bit grander, eh? Cavalry and Guards club, or suchlike?'

'I really did not know what to expect, Major.'

Wheatley stifled a belch. 'I've been black-balled in most of those places,' he said. 'Not quite the right sort, you see. But that doesn't bother me. Full of chinless wonders, and you can't get draught beer in them. Some of them even have a rule about not talking. Not talking! The only point in a rule like that would be if I could bring the wife, but they won't allow that either!'

Shaw smiled. The man had lost none of his disregard for social niceties since they had last met.

Over lunch they talked mostly of trivial matters; half an hour later they had finished, and Shaw emptied the last drops of his pint of beer (Wheatley had consumed three). The two men now sat back, replete; Shaw lit his pipe and Wheatley lit a cigarette.

'Now then, Mr Shaw,' said Wheatley, 'I daresay you didn't come here on a social call, so perhaps we ought to get down to business. What's on your mind?'

Shaw briefly summarised the events of the last couple of days, showing Wheatley the evidence gathered by Ludd. Wheatley puffed intently on his cigarette as he looked down at the photograph of Eleanor.

'Hmm, pretty girl,' he said. 'You can tell that even though she's dead. Now who would want to go and kill someone as pretty as that?'

'I rather hoped you might be able to help answer that,' said Shaw. 'We appear to have been rebuffed by the police in no uncertain terms.'

'Yes, that's enough to set alarm bells ringing, if you ask me,' said Wheatley. 'It suggests there's more to this than meets the eye, and it either involves the police themselves, or certain parties who have sufficient clout to tell the police what to do. Now, you say this asylum place…'

'Ravenswood,'

'This Ravenswood place, is questionable, because of what your doctor pal found out.'

'Correct.'

'That suggests to me it's not the police themselves that want you to forget about Miss Harrington, because they messed up, or something; it indicates that it's some other people who are able to order the police around.'

'I take it you mean…influential people,' said Shaw.

'That's exactly what I mean. And the order didn't come from me, if that's what you're thinking. This Chief Inspector Ludd, is he reliable?'

'I should say completely reliable. Only he has been told to have no further part in the investigation.'

'I see,' said Wheatley, draining the last of his beer and smacking his lips. 'For now, I suggest you don't mention any of this to anyone, including the Chief Inspector. Have you told anyone else about our little meeting?'

'No,' said Shaw. 'Although my wife has her suspicions…'

'Don't they always!' barked Wheatley, roaring with laughter. 'Well, tell her what your conscience will let you, but don't involve anyone else, eh?'

Shaw nodded, and watched as Wheatley scooped up the brown envelopes from the table and shuffled them together. 'I'll take care of these for now. Now, Mr Shaw, I suggest you go home and forget all about this for a few days while I make some enquiries. I'll be seeing you.'

Chapter Four

Shaw made his way back to Liverpool Street Station on the Underground. He realised he was close to the westbound platform where Eleanor Harrington had met her demise, and curiosity got the better of him. He walked on to the platform, expecting some sort of cordon, but there was nothing; not even a police constable on point duty. There was nothing to suggest that only a short while ago, a living, breathing human being had suddenly been summoned to stand before her maker in the most violent of ways.

He felt a surge of pity, and said a brief prayer for her. Then he raised his head as he heard a voice behind him.

'I say, guv'nor, you don't want to hang about there too long. People 'as a way of getting' 'emselves killed if they stands there.'

Shaw looked up to see a wizened, stooped man of about sixty years of age, talking without removing the stub of a lighted cigarette from his mouth. He was dressed in railway uniform and carried a large broom.

'Ah, yes,' said Shaw. 'I read about that in the newspapers. Most regrettable. An accident, they say.'

'Accident, my…foot, guv'nor. I mean, vicar.'

Shaw realised the man had noticed his clerical collar, at which point his manner seemed to become more effusive. Shaw was used to this phenomenon; some people seemed willing to confide all manner of things to a clergyman that they would never dare speak of to a layman.

'Did you witness the occurrence?' asked Shaw with interest.

'Course I did,' said the little man. 'I was up there, weren't I? Sweeping down them steps.' He pointed to a flight of stairs that led to street level. 'By rights I shouldn't have been up there 'cos I don't work nights but I was covering for a bloke what couldn't make it that night. So there I was, and I seen the 'ole thing. Terrible, it was.'

'And you believe Miss Harrington's death was...not...an accident?' asked Shaw.

'That 'er name?' asked the man. '"Ow d'you know that? P'lice said as she was hanonymous.'

'I met her briefly in a professional capacity,' said Shaw carefully.

'You knew 'er? Then 'ow did you know she'd been killed when 'er name weren't in the papers?' asked the man suspiciously.

'I cannot be certain, but I believe it was her,' said Shaw. 'For reasons I cannot divulge at present.'

This seemed to intrigue the man, and he leaned forward on his broom and lowered his voice.

'I'd swear my davy on it she was pushed,' he said. The cigarette in his mouth had now burned down to about a quarter of an inch in length, and he deftly extinguished it and put it in his pocket, presumably, thought Shaw, to re-use the remaining tobacco.

'A great big 'ulking feller came up behind that girl, see,' continued the man, 'and he laid 'is 'ands on 'er.

Then that train come through the tunnel – and they comes through *fast* – like a rat up a drainpipe, so they do.'

As if to illustrate his point, a train roared past them, appearing as if out of nowhere from the darkness of the tunnel entrance.

Shaw stepped back quickly, but the man did not move a muscle, and remained leaning on his broom.

'And next thing she was under it,' he continued, 'and that was the end of 'er. Reckon she never felt a thing, and that's something to be thankful for, but garn, you should 'ave 'eard the screams of them as saw it 'appen.'

'Yes, I can imagine,' said Shaw with a shudder. 'You have, I take it, told all this to the police.'

'Course I did,' said the man. 'But they said as everyone what was around the poor girl thought she just fell; lorst her balance, like. Well, that was most likely on account of it was such a crush down there and they couldn't see anything 'cept the back of the 'ead of 'oo was in front of them, and most of them was 'alf cut anyway. But I was up there, you see.'

The man pointed again to the staircase, and continued.

'And I 'ad what you might call a grandstand view, see, an' you can put a Bible in me 'and 'ere and now, and I'll swear that feller *pushed* her.'

'Didn't the police believe you saw that she was pushed?' asked Shaw.

'They was hinterested at first,' said the man, 'and they arst me to come back to give a proper statement, like. But when I went and gone to the p'lice station, they said not to worry, it were an accident and I won't be needed at no coroner's 'earing thank you very much, and me taken 'alf 'our out of me dinner time!'

'I see,' said Shaw. 'Could you describe the man that you say pushed her?'

The man took a packet of five cigarettes from his top pocket and put one in his mouth, then fumbled for a match. Shaw obliged him with a light, and he nodded his thanks, exhaling a long stream of smoke.

'Well now,' said the man, ''e was wearing a cap, 'an from up them stairs I couldn't see 'is face 'cos the angle was wrong. But 'e was big. Six-an'-'alf foot tall I should say, with great big 'ands, like 'eavyweight boxer. Matter of fact, 'e 'ad a cauliflower ear, an' all. Maybe 'e *was* a boxer.'

'Hi, stop slacking there,' came a shout from the opposite platform. Shaw saw a uniformed man gesticulating at them, with an angry expression on his face.

'That's my guv'nor,' said the sweeper. 'I'd best get a move on. But if you knowed that young girl I'd say you ought to tell the law what I told you. They might take more notice of a gentleman, than the likes of me.'

'I may well do that,' said Shaw. 'It is possible I may be able to find the man who you say pushed her.'

Shaw reached in his pocket and held out a shilling to the man. 'You have been most helpful. Perhaps you would take something in return, Mr...?'

'They just calls me Mitch,' said the man, who began sweeping the platform and speaking out of the side of his mouth, presumably in the hope of fooling his gimlet-eyed superior who was watching from across the tracks.

65

'And you can put that money in your church poor-box,' he added. 'I can see as you're an 'onourable sort of gent. If you wants to do something for me, you find that big feller an' see 'im 'anged for what 'e done.'

The man hurried off, sweeping as he went, and made furtive glances across the platform to check the movements of his superior. Shaw walked up to the mainline terminus and strode across the concourse to his waiting train. Then he stopped.

'An 'onourable gent,' the sweeper had called him. Of course! Why hadn't he thought of that before? He hurried out of the terminus and asked a policeman the way to the nearest public library. Soon he was seated at a scarred municipal table with a copy of *Burke's Peerage* in front of him. The book appeared hardly used, and he looked round at his fellow readers and realised why. It was a poor district, and most of the occupants of the library seemed to be there chiefly to escape the cold weather. They had little need, he assumed, for books on honorifics.

He thumbed through the large tome and confirmed what he had dimly known already; 'Honourable' was a courtesy title afforded to the daughters of viscounts and barons. Eleanor, he recalled, had mentioned it off-hand when Keating had asked her name.

Shaw wondered if the woman had done that deliberately to ensure she could be identified should anything befall her, without appearing too obvious about it. It was a simple matter of checking all the Harringtons in the index. It did not take long; there were only three listed and the final entry described 'Harrington, John Frederick Tolmers, 16th Baron

Stoneleigh', followed by details of the nobleman's various other honours, his London and country addresses and family members. The 'heir and spare' – the man's two sons – were listed, and then his daughter, the honourable Eleanor Lucinda Harrington, born 1911.

Shaw noted down the addresses and closed the book loudly, causing some of the down-at-heel readers to look up curiously. He then jumped up and hurried into the street. Throwing caution to the winds he hailed a taxi, and directed it to Belgravia. Of course, it was not yet the Season, and the house might not even be occupied, but it was worth a try.

Fifteen minutes later, he mounted the steps of a large, white wedding-cake of a house overlooking a private square where the trees were just starting to bud. He rang the bell and within a few moments an immaculately dressed butler opened the door and looked him up and down with a rapid critical eye.

'Yes?'

'Good day to you,' said Shaw. 'May I speak to Baron Stoneleigh?'

The butler raised an eyebrow. 'May I ask what it is in connection with, sir?'

'A family matter,' said Shaw simply.

'Your name, sir?'

Shaw fumbled for a card, and gave it to the servant, who looked at it briefly then placed it carefully in his waistcoat pocket. 'One moment sir,' he said, and the door was closed.

Shaw suddenly realised that Eleanor's parents might not actually know their daughter was dead. Did they even know she had been kept in some sort of asylum?

Mindful of Major Wheatley's advice not to pursue the matter at present, he suddenly wished he had not rung the bell of this particular house.

The door re-opened, and the butler, as passive as ever, simply said 'His lordship is not at home,' and began to close the door.

'I don't quite understand,' said Shaw. 'Not at home as in, not at home, or not at home as in, his Lordship does not wish to see me?'

The butler gave an almost inaudible sniff at such a blatant questioning of social euphemism, and began to close the door. Shaw pressed against it and spoke rapidly, taking a gamble on what he was about to say.

'I have just noticed you are wearing a mourning armband,' he said, 'and that the blinds of the house are all drawn. Can you please tell his Lordship that I may know something about his daughter's death?'

The door slammed shut. Shaw breathed out slowly, then turned to walk down the flight of steps to the street. Just as he reached the pavement, the door re-opened.

'Will you come this way, sir?' said the butler.

A few moments later Shaw was seated in an enormous, shadowy drawing room, the windows of which were largely obscured by venetian blinds, drawn down as a sign of respect for the dead. John Harrington, Baron Stoneleigh, dressed in deepest mourning, looked down at him accusingly as he paced up and down the immense rug on the floor. His white moustache bristled and, thought, Shaw, the only thing missing from his portrayal of a stage aristocrat was a monocle.

'Now sir,' said the Baron, 'When Herrick gave me your card I assumed it was for some sort of subscription.

Missions, or some such. We already give to a number of those. Then I overheard you say something about my daughter. Well, what is it you want to tell me?'

'May I first offer my condolences,' said Shaw. 'On your recent bereavement.'

'No sir, you may not,' bridled the Baron. 'I don't know you from Adam, so I won't take any parson's platitudes from you about my family. I'll ask again. What do you know about my daughter?'

Shaw realised there was no point trying to tread carefully with this man, so he decided to jump in head first.

'I believe she may have been murdered.'

'Then you're mistaken, sir. The police and half a dozen witnesses say it was an accident. Why should you know any different? And how do you know about this anyway? I was strictly assured that my daughter's name would be kept out of the pape…'

The Baron paused, as if wary of revealing something, and he fixed Shaw with a beady eye. 'Look here,' he continued, 'just who are you?'

'Lord Stoneleigh,' said Shaw, 'were you aware that your daughter had been kept in some sort of private asylum?'

Shaw guessed by the man's impassive reaction that he had been well aware of that fact.

'I *asked* you, sir, who the devil are you?' he demanded. 'Who are you working for? Some sort of private enquiry agent? I'll wager you're not even a real clergyman. Are you from the press? A muckraker, eh? Get out!'

The Baron crossed to the chimneypiece and pressed the electric bell to summon the servants.

'Your daughter came to me in fear of her life,' said Shaw rapidly, conscious that he did not have much time. 'There were three men pursuing her, whom I believe to have come from the Ravenswood private asylum in Suffolk. One of those men was seen very close to your daughter moments before her death at Liverpool Street sta…'

'This gentleman is leaving,' snapped the Baron, cutting Shaw off as the butler entered the room.

'Very good sir,' said the butler, and stepped between Shaw and the Baron.

'If you wish to speak to me, my address and telephone number are on my card,' said Shaw quickly, but the butler gently took hold of his arm and guided him to the door.

'*This* way sir,' he said firmly.

Shaw conceded, but as he left the room under the haughty gaze of the Baron, he heard a click and saw a small door to the right of the chimneypiece shut, as if someone had been listening.

For three days, life went on as normal for Shaw. He continued his usual round of services, house visits and meetings. His wife knew him well enough not to ask him what had happened in London, and Keating was presumably too busy with his new board practice to pay social calls, so he did not discuss the matter of Eleanor's death with anybody. Yet it weighed heavily on his mind. He scolded himself for not predicting her escape from the bathroom window. If only he had...but it was no use. All he could do now was wait.

He did not have to wait long. The day after he returned from London, the telephone rang and Hettie came into his study.

'Please sir,' she said, 'but it's a telephone call for you. A London caller.'

Shaw picked up the receiver.

'Is that Reverend Shaw?'

The long-distance line crackled. It was an aristocratic sounding voice that Shaw had not heard before, and yet, there was something familiar about it. It reminded him of Eleanor.

'This is Reverend Shaw speaking. May I assume this is Lady Stoneleigh? Eleanor's mother?'

'You are correct. Fortunately the fire was not lit when my husband threw your card into the grate, and I was able to extract it. I apologise for his conduct yesterday but as I am sure you will understand, the news of our daughter's death has been a great shock.'

'That is perfectly understandable. I take it you were listening at the door of the drawing room?'

There was a pause, and Shaw wondered if he had offended the woman.

'My husband refused to let me see you. If he knew I was speaking to you on the telephone he would be most upset. Mr Shaw, I shall be brief. Whatever evidence you think you have uncovered about poor Eleanor, I strongly advise you to forget about it. Please do not cause others...or yourself...pain by raking over the past.'

'My dear Lady Stoneleigh,' said Shaw carefully, 'I

have reason to believe your daughter's death was not accidental. If you…'

'I shan't tell you again,' said Lady Stoneleigh, with a note of command in her voice; but Shaw noticed a note of fear also. 'No good will come of your involvement, so please, for your own sake if nobody else's, *stay out of this matter.*'

'But…' began Shaw, and then stopped as he heard a dry click on the line. She had hung up.

Shaw frowned as he replaced the telephone receiver. If Lady Stoneleigh had thought her call would put an end to his interest in her late daughter, she was wrong. It had had quite the opposite effect.

Nurse Jane Reeves stood in front of Dr Landis in his luxuriantly furnished office at Ravenswood. She was not the sort of person to frighten easily, but she felt a tremor of unease as her superior looked her up and down from behind his desk.

'I think you know what this is about,' he said.

'If you would allow me to explain, doctor…' she began firmly.

'No thank you,' said Landis, raising his hand. 'It is quite clear to me where the problem lies. I should never have conceded to your suggestion that Miss Harrington was sufficiently harmless to allow you to enter her room alone.'

'I realise that now, doctor.'

'I take a certain amount of responsibility for that

myself,' continued the doctor, 'and also for changing her medication from intravenous to oral administration. But you must take some responsibility in that regard also. I presume she somehow managed to trick you into thinking she had taken her pills, when she had not? Otherwise she would not have been physically capable of making her escape.'

'I don't know how she did it, doctor,' protested Reeves, with a scowl on her face. 'She was a very troublesome patient, and as you can see she didn't hesitate to use violence.' Here she pointed to the sticking plaster on her temple, which Landis gave but a cursory glance.

'I can perhaps overlook some of your failings, Miss Reeves,' said the doctor, 'but what I cannot overlook is the fact that you left your keys away from your person, and not only that, it seems you had your car key in the same bunch. That really was most irresponsible. If Barton had not been passing and seen you unconscious on the floor, raising the alarm, Miss Harrington might have completely evaded us. '

'I'm sorry, doctor,' said Reeves, but she did not sound apologetic, and stared into the middle distance beyond the doctor's head. It was almost an expression of 'dumb insolence' and Landis noticed.

'I am tempted to give you notice,' he said, 'but up until now your record, at least here, has been exemplary. I am sure you are aware it is difficult to find nursing staff able and willing to undertake...this sort of work. Consider this a severe warning. If anything like this happens again, the consequences for you will be severe.'

Reeves nodded curtly but said nothing.

'In future you will not enter any patient's room unless an orderly is with you,' continued Landis. 'Is that clear?'

'Perfectly, doctor.'

'You may go.'

'Dr Landis, has Miss Harrington been apprehended?'

The doctor looked disapprovingly at Reeves.

'That is none of your concern now. Suffice to say she is no longer able to cause us any difficulties.'

A knowing look crossed Reeves' face.

'I understand, doctor. Oh, but one more thing before I go. About the mechanic you arranged to recover my motor car. He has most kindly loaned me another until mine can be repaired, but I shall need his name and address for the insurance company.'

'Don't worry about any of that,' said Landis, showing Reeves to the door. 'You shan't need to involve insurance companies. I shall take care of it, just as I took care of Miss Harrington's unfortunate escapade. Now, I think you had better check on the patients. We don't want any further…escapades, do we?'

Reeves smiled grimly, and left the room.

On Friday a small envelope arrived in the post at the vicarage, containing a simple handwritten note: 'Meet me at Netley Golf Club, 3pm, Saturday. Yrs, A.J.W.'

Wheatley, Shaw remembered, did not trust the telephone, and presumably he did not trust post-cards either. Feeling rather self-conscious, Shaw put the letter on the fire before anyone else could see it, although he was not quite sure why.

On Saturday afternoon he bicycled to Netley Golf Club, a mock-tudor building nestled amongst what passed for rolling hills in Suffolk, next to an estate of new semi-detached villas which stretched half a mile or so into the market town of Great Netley.

He found Wheatley in a quiet corner of the bar, with a pint of beer in front of him.

'Ah, Mr Shaw,' said Wheatley brightly. 'Not a bad little course they have here. Managed to get nine holes in. I didn't invite you along as I assumed you weren't a golfer. Was I right?'

Shaw breathed a sigh of relief. He had been rather worried that Wheatley was going to insist on them traipsing about the course while he flailed around amateurishly with a set of borrowed clubs.

'I have…dabbled…but it is not a game I have much time for,' said Shaw.

'Of course, I wouldn't expect it of a high-minded man such as yourself,' said Wheatley amiably. 'I find it's the only time I get to relax,' he added. 'I hadn't played this course before so I thought I'd motor down for the day and kill two birds with one stone, so to speak. Three birds, come to think of it. Do sit down. Glass of beer?'

'It is a little early for me,' said Shaw as he sat down, 'but thank you all the same.'

'Suit yourself,' said Wheatley as took a large sip of beer.

'Have you any news?' asked Shaw.

'Ah, now, it's been a rather eventful few days,' said Wheatley enthusiastically. 'I've been making a few…discreet enquiries…about our Miss Harrington, and this Ravenswood place. And I don't like what I've found.'

Wheatley looked around the room briefly, but it was empty apart from a barman at the far end of the room polishing glasses. Through the leaded windows Shaw could see a group of men crowding around the first tee, and then he heard the distant thwack of a golf ball.

'You'll understand Mr Shaw,' continued Wheatley, 'that in my department we've ways and means of finding out most things. Ways and means not open to the police, for example.'

'I understand,' said Shaw.

'Of course. But when I started asking around about this matter, I came up against what I can only describe as evasiveness. We know a bit about this Dr Landis who runs Ravenswood, but there are a few gaps in his *bona fides* that worry me. Not to mention other things. Missing records, people refusing to speak to me on the telephone, secretaries saying their bosses were not in the office when I knew for a fact they were. And there were two deaths in Ravenswood that didn't strike me as altogether above-board.'

Here Wheatley consulted a small notebook which Shaw noticed did not contain handwriting, but some sort of shorthand or code. 'A man called James Phillipson and a woman called Ursula DeVere died there in the last year. By rights, there should have been an inquest but it looks as if someone blocked it. You get my point?'

'I think so,' said Shaw. 'A conspiracy of some sort?'

'You might call it that,' said Wheatley. 'And what's more, I found out your Miss Harrington wasn't just an ordinary miss. She was the…'

'The Honourable Eleanor Harrington', interrupted Shaw.

'How did you know that?'

Shaw related his conversation with the station cleaner, his meeting with Lord Stoneleigh, and the telephone conversation with Lady Stoneleigh.

Wheatley frowned and took another sip of beer. 'I think I did tell you not to do anything in regards to this matter until I had had a chance to ask around, did I not?'

'You did. But I chanced to meet a witness to Miss Harrington's death and…'

'And one thing led to another. All right Mr Shaw, you don't have to apologise to me. Matter of fact I'm impressed you worked out who she was, because it shows you have the sort of skills that I require.'

'I don't follow.'

'Mr Shaw, do you want to get to the bottom of what happened to Miss Harrington, and perhaps stop it happening to others?'

'Of course,' said Shaw. 'But I thought that you were to investigate the…'

'I've gone about as far as I can without being noticed,' interrupted Wheatley. 'And people in my line of work can't afford to be noticed. All I've been able to establish is there's *something* rum about that Ravenswood place, but not exactly *what*. The police won't get anywhere with it. What I need is a man on the inside. And that's where I think you can help.'

'You mean…you wish me to pose as a…a lunatic?' asked Shaw in bewilderment.

Wheatley laughed uproariously, a laugh which then descended into an attack of smoker's cough, and he paused to take a large sip of beer, then wiped his eyes.

'Oh Lor, that's a good one,' said Wheatley.

'Major Wheatley,' said Shaw, 'I fail to see what is so amus…'

'I'm sorry, Mr Shaw,' interrupted Wheatley. 'Don't mind me. I just had visions of you trying to act like a lunatic in a straitjacket. You're about the sanest person I've ever met!'

'I assume that is a compliment,' said Shaw.

'I most certainly don't want you to act like a lunatic,' continued the Major. 'What I'm asking…suggesting, is that you simply do your job.'

'I'm afraid I still don't follow.'

'Are you sure those three lackeys that were after Miss Harrington didn't see you?'

'Quite certain. I was in the dining room the whole time they were at the door. But what of it?'

'All in good time, Mr Shaw,' said Wheatley. 'The Ravenswood asylum is private, but it's still administered by a board of directors. Now, that lot were obstructive when I talked to them in the guise of a sort of government inspector, but I didn't get the impression they were hiding anything. They're the sort of do-gooding charitable types who don't know – or don't *want* to know – that rum stuff is going on below them, and the people below them make sure they're kept in the dark. One thing I did establish is they're not keeping to the conditions of their administrative trust, which is that they must employ a Church of England chaplain.'

'I see,' said Shaw. 'But I don't think I have the time

to…'

'That's the beauty of it,' said Wheatley. 'It doesn't have to be a full time job. He's just supposed to visit a minimum of once a week and provide Holy Communion and so on. You could manage that, couldn't you?'

Shaw thought for a moment. 'I do not have too many commitments on Wednesdays. I could bicycle there quite easily, and…'

'That's that then,' said Wheatley. 'You can go there once a week – more if you can spare the time – and get to know what's going on. Talk to the patients, and the staff and what not. Get a feeling for the place. If you can find any evidence – firm evidence, mind, written documents and so on – that there's anything out of order there, my chaps will take over and deal with it. How does that sound?'

Shaw thought back to the warning he had received on the telephone from Lady Stoneleigh, and he bridled.

'Of course I shall do it,' he said. 'But the bishop…'

'Your bishop,' said Wheatley with a chuckle, 'has a most impressive golf handicap. I took the trouble to visit him in Midchester this morning and when I saw the clubs in his study, we got on like a house on fire. He's happy for you to become the Ravenswood chaplain.'

'You mean the Bishop of Midchester was willing to enter into a conspiracy with some sort of…of…secret agent?'

'Hush!' said Wheatley, glancing over to the door as a noisy group of golfers entered the bar. 'I don't go around announcing myself as a "secret agent" as you call it. As far as that bishop knows, he met with the representative of Ravenswood's charitable trust. If you're in agreement I'll send a letter to Landis telling them to expect you and no ifs or buts. Now, what do you say to the proposal?'

'I say yes,' replied Shaw firmly.

'Good man,' said Wheatley. 'Oh, and sign this will you?'

He pushed forward a sheet of foolscap paper.

'If this is the Official Secrets Act,' said Shaw, 'I have already signed it.'

'Don't worry about that old guff,' said Wheatley dismissively. 'This is far more important. Your expense allowance.'

'What on earth...?'

'You're co-opted as a temporary member of my department while you're working up at Ravenswood. That entitles you to claim expenses...now let me see...' Wheatley squinted at the dense wording on the form. 'Ah yes. Ten shillings per day plus travel expenses of...I know it says bicycles here somewhere...yes...one penny per mile for cycles. I doubt they've raised that since the blasted things were invented. Plus up to half-a-crown for meals if you need them. Sign there.'

'Major Wheatley, I have no desire to...'

'Spare me the noble act, Mr Shaw. This is all coming out of your taxes so you might as well get something back. Put it towards a new steeple, or Bibles for Abyssinia or whatever it is your lot use money for.'

Shaw sighed, and signed the form.

'I'll be seeing you then, Mr Shaw,' said Wheatley, standing up. 'And for God's sake, be *careful*.'

Ruth Leigh-Ellison sat in the day room at Ravenswood, staring out into the damp, shadowy garden. A slight, pretty woman in her mid twenties with refined features and a pleasant, almost musical voice, she drifted as usual in and out of sleep, and struggled to retain a coherent chain of thought. She could not remember exactly how long she had been like this, nor exactly how long she had been in this place, nor even exactly what the place was.

The room was sparsely decorated and furnished. There were no ornaments, only some institutional furniture, most of which was bolted to the floor. There were no paintings on the walls, nor were there any mirrors. No flowers. How she missed flowers! She remembered lots of them, bunches and bunches, and cards too, on her birthday after her first Season…but then something had happened which she could no longer remember, and there had been no more flowers.

She looked around at the other people in the room; half a dozen or so of them. One or two stared vacantly at jigsaw puzzles on a table; another fidgeted, talking to himself; two more simply stared into space as she herself did most of the time. There was something she was trying to remember. What was it? Was someone missing? Somebody should be here who wasn't, but she could not work out who it might be.

'Now then Ruth,' came a bright voice next to her. 'Time for your afternoon pill.'

Ruth turned to see who it was. She remembered her. That bustling, over-efficient nurse with the common-prim voice who never stopped talking; one never knew if she was going to be nice or nasty.

'Don't want it,' said Ruth forcefully.

The nurse glanced over to the orderly who stood in the corner watching over the room. He was a large, heavily built man with a cauliflower ear. Ruth remembered she did not like him either. She did not like him *at all*.

'We're not going to be difficult, are we?' said the nurse. 'Just one pill now, not two as before. The doctor thinks you're getting better. Now be a good girl and take it.'

'No.'

'We don't want to have to ask Barton to help, do we?'

Barton. Ruth remembered who that was, and looked over at the big man in the corner of the room. He leered at her, and began to approach her. She snatched the pill from the metal tray that the nurse held out, and popped it into her mouth.

'There, that wasn't too difficult was it?' exclaimed the nurse, as she gave Ruth a sip of water from a metal beaker.

'Thank you Barton, we shan't need you,' she said in a colder tone to the orderly who had approached them. He shrugged, looked Ruth up and down as if she were a joint of meat hanging in a butcher's shop, and returned to his place in the corner of the room.

'Now you have a nice long sleep,' said the nurse, 'and I'll see you again in the evening for your next pill.'

Ruth waited until the nurse had gone, and when she

was sure that Barton wasn't looking, she deftly removed the pill from under her tongue and flicked it into a darkened corner of the room, where it landed silently out of sight.

Chapter Five

On the following Monday, Shaw bicycled four miles or so out of his village towards the neighbouring parish of Addenham Magna. It was another bright, sunny morning with the promise of spring in the air, and he looked admiringly up at the long tunnel of bare trees above him, which bore the light dusting of green that indicated the very first appearance of spring buds.

At morning service the previous day, Keating had asked if he had heard any news about the Harrington affair, and Shaw simply said that the matter was under investigation by the relevant authorities. He had also received a telephone call from Chief Inspector Ludd this morning, asking in a roundabout way what was going on, but Shaw simply gave the same answer he had given Keating. Ludd had grunted, and said 'I just hope you know what you're doing.'

Eventually, at the end of a long incline, Shaw saw Ravenswood, set back from the road under a canopy of thick, dark evergreens. He rarely had cause to come this far out of the village, although strictly speaking he, or at least his curate, ought to have called from time to time because it was just within the boundaries of his parish.

But the great and good that lived in large, remote houses far from villages did not, in Shaw's experience, always welcome the uninvited appearance of clergy at their gates. He dimly remembered it had been inhabited some years ago by two spinster sisters of very Victorian aspect, but that it had lain empty for some time after their deaths.

He propped his bicycle against the high front wall which separated the grounds from the lane, and rang the bell at the gate. The heavy-set porter seemed to have expected him, and said nothing more than 'go straight up, vicar,' pointing his thumb in the direction of the house after he unlocked the heavy gates.

When he reached the large stone portico of the house, the gloom seemed to deepen, and he felt a long way away from the brightness of the lane. The trunks of the pine trees and the grey stone of the house itself were dusted with green, but it was the green of mould rather than spring buds. The only sound was that of rooks cawing in some nearby field.

There was much clattering of bolts and bars and then the large front door opened. A large man, who might almost have been the double of the one at the gate, save that the head of this latter man was completely bald and, Shaw noticed, he had a cauliflower ear, with a small scar above it on the side of his head. Was this the man who…? Shaw felt a sudden tremor of unease, and shook it off by smiling brightly.

'Good morning,' he said. 'My name is Lucian Shaw. I believe you are expecting me.'

The giant looked at him blankly. For a moment, Shaw thought he recognised him and, likewise, he saw a flicker of recognition on the man's face. Had they met somewhere before? It seemed unlikely. Any further speculation was postponed as the giant stepped aside and a smaller man appeared, who pulled the door open a little wider. He had neatly combed, heavily brilliantined hair and had a dapper air about him and something, thought Shaw, of the racing fraternity, though that seemed at odds with his rather severe looking uniform tunic.

'Come in vicar,' he said, with an attempt at levity. 'Don't mind my associates here, they're not used to company. Well, not respectable company anyway.'

'My name's Chivers, Freddie Chivers,' said the man, offering his hand to Shaw. His grasp was firm and Shaw let it go quickly, realising he recognised the nasal voice as the same he had heard while listening from the dining room at Keating's house.

He gestured for Shaw to enter. 'I'm head orderly here. This here's Joe Barton' – he gestured to the cauliflower eared man, who continued to stare blankly at Shaw. Famous, he is. A celebrity, you might say.'

'Leave off Freddie,' growled the man.

'No, straight up,' said Chivers. 'Boxer, he was. British heavyweight contender, 1928. Got beaten by Phil Scott on points up White City. I lost ten bob on that!'

Had that been why Shaw had recognised him, he wondered? But Shaw could not recall ever having attended a boxing match. He had boxed himself at Cambridge, but thereafter lost interest in the sport. Had he seen Barton in the newsreels or newspapers perhaps? It seemed unlikely that the man should stick in his mind if that was the only place he had seen his image.

'And him at the gate is Gauge,' continued Chivers.' Oh and by the way, I hope you don't mind if we don't join in with any of your prayer meetings. See, Barton and Gauge are what you might call free-thinkers, and I'm a Jehovah's Witness.'

'Indeed?' said Shaw.

'Nah,' replied Chivers with a rasping laugh. 'I only told 'em that when I got called up, so's the army wouldn't take me!'

He laughed uproariously, seemingly oblivious to Shaw's look of distaste.

'I am surprised that enabled you to avoid fighting,' he said.

'Well I wasn't one of those conchies who just sat the war out in prison,' said Chivers indignantly. 'I had to work in a hospital for soldiers gone doolally, so I saw plenty of action, but against me own blooming side!'

He chuckled and gestured for Shaw to follow him across a wide hallway with a tiled floor and a sweeping staircase. It must have been a grand entrance in its day, thought Shaw, but now had a tired, institutional look, with paint peeling from the walls, and various official additions such as fire buckets and bars on the windows.

'This here's the chief's office,' he said, and knocked on a large door, then opened it.

'New padre to see you, doctor,' said Chivers, who winked at Shaw and then left the room.

Shaw looked across the large, luxuriantly furnished office which was in stark contrast to the bleakness of the hallway. There was a fire burning brightly in the grate, and watery sunlight had even managed to penetrate through the French doors, which were unbarred.

A man in a white medical coat was standing behind a handsome antique desk, and next to him was a small but solid and intimidating looking woman in some sort of nurse's uniform.

'Good morning, Mr Shaw,' said the man. 'My name is Dr Landis. This is my assistant, Miss Reeves.'

'How do you do,' said Shaw.

'Sit down please,' said Landis as he himself sat down, but Shaw noticed that Reeves remained standing and stared sullenly at him.

'Now then,' said Landis, looking at a typewritten letter on his desk, 'I see you are to be our new chaplain. It seems I had overlooked a technicality in the overseers' regulations which states you are a legal requirement. Your bishop kindly wrote to me to point out my error.'

'So I understand,' said Shaw.

'Though how the bishop knew we had not been able to find a suitable chaplain, I cannot imagine.'

'Something to do with the governing body of this establishment, I presume?' asked Shaw.

'Perhaps so,' said Landis. 'No matter. I had rather hoped that running a private establishment would make it less likely for bureaucratic interference in my work,' said the doctor, 'but it seems this is now the way things are done and we must bear it with good grace.'

'Indeed,' said Shaw. 'I hope that you will consider my addition to your staff not to be "bureaucratic interference" but a help, rather than a hindrance.'

Landis put down the letter and looked at Shaw intently. There was something deeply unsettling, he thought, in the way his grey eyes bored into his own.

'Let me be frank, Mr Shaw,' he said. 'I am not a religious man. In fact, I consider religion to be one of the chief causes of disquiet in wider society, and of psychological disturbances in the individual. Does that shock you?'

'It is hardly a radical notion these days, Dr Landis,' replied Shaw, determined to match the man's probing gaze.

'Perhaps not...' said the doctor, 'but it is the truth, nevertheless.'

'There we must agree to disagree,' said Shaw carefully.

'No matter,' said Landis again with a rigid smile, as he stood up. 'You let me do my work, and I shall let you do yours, Mr Shaw, and the board of directors above me, and the functionaries above them, shall be kept happy. Now, do you know much about our work here?'

'Not a great deal,' said Shaw. 'I believe you are a small, private establishment giving care to lunatics.'

'We do not use that term,' warned Landis. 'We prefer to call them residents here. And we do not just give care, Mr Shaw. We transform broken human beings into whole ones again, just as your church liked to think it did in years past. The difference is, what we do, *works*. Come, let me show you around.'

Landis led the way into the hall and Shaw followed, with Reeves behind him. He could not help feeling a slight sense of unease at the regular tapping sound of her severe black shoes on the tiled floor, and he was relieved when they entered a large, carpeted drawing room.

'Ah, good, everyone seems to be here,' said Landis.

Shaw looked around to see six people seated in institutional chairs which appeared to be bolted to the floor; some read books, others looked listlessly at jigsaw puzzles, while others simply stared out through the barred French doors into the gloomy, shadowed garden. Shaw had been expecting an atmosphere of torment – of evil, perhaps, in this place, but instead he felt nothing but a blank neutrality, a complete absence of any feelings whatsoever, as if human emotion simply had ceased to exist. He noticed the large orderly, Barton, was eyeing him coldly from the corner, and on the other side of the room sat Chivers in an armchair, smoking a cigarette listlessly and examining his finger-nails.

'You have met Barton and Chivers,' said Landis, and moved on to introducing Shaw to the patients around the room.

'Mr Murchison, Miss Layton, Mrs Dalby, Commander Elphick, Mr Grant.'

Shaw greeted them cordially, but none seemed particularly responsive, and they either ignored him or gave vague greetings, then lost interest. Only one person seemed to have any sort of lucidity; a young woman with close-cropped hair and intelligent eyes, who made some effort to focus on Shaw when he looked at her.

'This is Miss Ruth Leigh-Ellison,' said Landis proudly. 'We have high hopes for her. This is the new chaplain, Mr Shaw.'

'How do you do ?' asked Shaw brightly.

The woman blinked rapidly and opened her mouth, but a few seconds went by before she spoke.

'How…do…you do?'

'I am very glad to make your acquaintance,' said Shaw. 'I hope I can count on your attendance when I administer Holy Communion here in a few days' time.'

The woman stared at Shaw blankly, but he sensed

there was some sort of understanding deep within the dark pools of her brown eyes. She nodded slowly.

'Very good,' said Shaw. 'I shall look forward to it.'

Landis seemed genuinely pleased at the woman's response, and then took Shaw's arm.

'Come along, Mr Shaw,' he said. 'I shall show you the rest of the premises.'

Once they were outside the sitting room, Shaw lowered his voice. 'Forgive me, Dr Landis,' he said, 'but you seem to have remarkably few staff. Yourself, Miss Reeves and the three orderlies. Is that all?'

Landis gave a dry chuckle. 'Were you envisioning violent patients who required four strong men each to control them?'

'Something of that sort, yes. I have had occasion to visit the county asylum, where…'

'My dear Mr Shaw,' interrupted Landis, 'we are not the county asylum and we do not require the barbaric, out-dated methods of control and restraint that they use. I employ a highly advanced method of treatment which does away with the need for all that.'

'Indeed?' said Shaw, and he recalled Keating's mention of the needle marks on Eleanor's arm. 'Some sort of…medicinal treatment, perhaps?'

'Not quite,' said Landis, 'but something along those lines. Now, come along.'

Landis led Shaw briskly around the house with Reeves always in the rear, her shoes tapping insistently on the stone floors wherever they went. Landis waved an arm at each room in turn.

'The dining room…the kitchens – we have a lady from the village who comes in daily to cook and clean.

Everyone else lives on the premises, including myself unless I am in Town, with the exception of Miss Reeves here, who lives some distance away. The orderlies' rooms and the bathrooms are upstairs, within easy reach of the residents' bedrooms.'

'And this room?' asked Shaw, putting his hand on the knob of a door close to the foot of the stairs.

'That…is of no concern to you,' said Landis, taking Shaw by the arm. 'Just a cellar. Now, may I offer you a glass of sherry?'

Shaw nodded, and Landis led him to his office. Before they entered he cast another glance at the door by the foot of the stairs, and then noticed Reeves looking at him with a dark-eyed intensity.

That evening, after the usual institutional meal in the dining room, Ruth sat in the drawing room and waited for Reeves to administer her pill. Could she risk the same trick again? She decided it was worth trying. After all, what could they do to her if they found out? Lock her up? What did that matter, when she was already a prisoner? She hid the pill under her tongue and, once Reeves had left, she quickly flicked it away under the heavy sofa in the corner. Its legs were bolted to the floor and she doubted anyone ever cleaned under there.

Now she had gone a whole day without her medication, she felt her mental fog clearing slightly, and her vision and hearing seemed to be improved also. It was as if she were waking up from a long sleep, but the process seemed to be taking hours rather than seconds.

She suddenly began to experience strange sensations. At first she thought they were hallucinations, but then she realised they were memories – or at least, snatches of memories, which danced upon her inward eye for a moment then disappeared. She could not remember the last time she had *really* remembered.

She looked around the empty drawing room. The other residents had each been escorted up to bed and she assumed she soon would be also. Then she heard a rattling sound in the corridor, and lowered voices.

She surprised herself by moving stealthily out of her chair to stand closer to the door. Her physical, as well as mental, agility seemed to be returning to her. Once she was close to the door, she opened it a crack and listened. She heard a low voice and realised it was Barton.

'We 'aven't taken that girl up yet,' he said. 'Doctor said not to do this until they'd all gone up.'

'Don't worry about it,' said another voice, which she recognised as Chivers'. 'That one's always so doped she'll barely be able to blink let alone move around and cause trouble. Gauge can put her to bed when he locks up. Let's face it, that's the nearest he'll ever get to taking a popsy to bed!' He laughed uproariously, then lowered his voice. 'The quicker we get this done the quicker we can get the card school started up in my room, eh?'

She shuddered at the thought of the lecherous Gauge manhandling her into bed. Had he ever…she struggled to think…no. She was fairly certain nothing like that had occurred here, but there was something…she shook her head as the brief spark of memory sputtered out.

Opening the door a crack, she saw the two orderlies

standing by the little door next to the main staircase. With them was a man in a wheelchair whom she recognised as one of the patients, Commander Elphick. He seemed barely conscious and his head lolled to one side.

'Upsy-daisy' said Barton, and lifted the man onto his shoulder in a fireman's lift, as if he were no heavier than a satchel.

'Get him all set up and I'll tell the doctor he's ready,' said Chivers. 'And don't be too long – I want to win back that five bob you had off me last night.'

Barton opened the cellar door with a creak, and disappeared down a flight of steps.

'Commander!' scoffed Chivers to himself as he closed the door. 'He won't be commanding anything no more, that's for sure.'

Two days later it was Wednesday and Shaw bicycled to Ravenswood to administer Holy Communion for the first time.

Landis greeted him cursorily, and retreated into his office, saying he had a lot of paperwork to carry out. Shaw politely nodded, and, knowing what his reply would be, did not even bother to invite the man to the service.

'You can set things up in the drawing room,' said Reeves as she clacked her way along the corridor beside Shaw.

'I can't say I think any of this is necessary,' she

snapped, 'as most of our patients are unlikely to comprehend what is going on. It may even disturb some of them.'

'Perhaps,' said Shaw. 'Or it may do them some good.'

Shaw entered the drawing room and Reeves clapped her hands twice. 'Now come along everybody,' she announced. 'You all remember Mr Shaw who came a few days ago, don't you?'

Shaw looked around and saw the people he recognised from his last visit. There were the three orderlies, standing like policemen on point duty at different places around the room. The patients sat around, as before, in dressing gowns, and most of them looked blankly at him. He tried to remember their names.

There was the young woman, Ruth Leigh something…Leigh-Ellison, that was it. She seemed to recognise him, and the flicker of a smile crossed her face. There was Mr Grant, a middle-aged man who fidgeted constantly and seemed unable to make eye contact with anyone; Miss Layton, the elderly, brittle spinster who gave him a wan smile, and florid Mrs Dalby, who greeted him with 'good morning, Ernest dear. And how are the geraniums?'

'This is Mr Shaw, the chaplain, not your husband,' said Reeves sharply. 'Perhaps you would get started?' she asked. 'We have an hour or so and then they shall have to be taken in to lunch.'

'Very well, Miss Reeves,' said Shaw. 'I shall use this table as my makeshift altar.' He crossed to an occasional table by the French doors; it was bolted to the floor but just about the same height as the altar in his own church.

He opened his knapsack and took out his little portable communion set, and began laying the table neatly.

'Is it permitted to light candles?' he asked.

'I don't see why not,' said Reeves. 'We don't have any pyromaniacs here.'

'Very well,' said Shaw, and lit two small candles, placing them carefully in little holders on each side of the table.

Then a thought struck him.

'Will Commander Elphick be joining us?' asked Shaw.

He noticed a glance flicker between Reeves and the orderlies, and then the nurse smiled.

'Commander Elphick is…ah…'

'Commander Elphick is dead,' came a voice from the back of the room, and Shaw looked up to see that Landis had walked in.

'Really, doctor,' hissed Reeves. 'The patients…'

'The patients ought to face reality, Miss Reeves,' he said with a thin smile. 'Isn't that what we keep them here for? "In the midst of life we are in death,"eh, Mr Shaw?'

Shaw cleared his throat and momentarily ceased the arrangement of his communion items on the table.

'How, ah, did it happen?' he asked, trying to keep his voice light. 'Commander Elphick's death.'

'His heart gave out,' said Landis airily. 'In addition to his…mental difficulties, he had chronic myocarditis – inflammation of the heart. He could have gone at any time.'

'I see,' said Shaw. 'If you are to join us, Dr Landis, perhaps I may begin?'

'Oh, be my guest,' said Landis dismissively. 'I shall

remain here in an observational capacity, but please – do not ask me to take part.'

'Very well,' said Shaw. He distributed little prayer books to the assembled company, but they either dropped them, or stared at them with disinterest. He noticed, however, that Ruth thumbed through the book, finding the right place before he had even announced the page number.

He began with the Lord's Prayer, and noticed he was the only person reciting it; the orderlies shifted uncomfortably on their feet, and Reeves and Landis simply stared blankly at him.

He came to the General Confession intended to be said by all present, but, since he was the only one saying it, he began to speed up his delivery.

'We do earnestly repent, and are heartily sorry for these our misdoings; the remembrance of them is grievous unto us; the burden of them is intolerable…'

He then looked over at Ruth and saw that she was whispering the words, a single tear rolling down her cheek.

When he came to administer the bread and wine, only one person came forward, and that was Ruth. She knelt before the table, holding her hands out before her.

'The body of our Lord Jesus Christ, which was shed for thee…'

Ruth reverently consumed the elements, replying 'amen' each time, and returned to her seat.

Shaw could not help noticing a look of fascination on Landis' face as he watched Ruth sit down.

When the service was over, the residents moved through to the dining room, and Landis approached

Shaw.

'Thank you, Mr Shaw,' he said. 'That was most interesting.'

'I thought that you believed religion to be the chief cause of disquiet in our society,' said Shaw.

'Indeed I do,' said Landis, 'but I am still a man of science. I was interested to see the effect of your little performance on the assembled company. Did you see the only person to take any notice was Miss Leigh-Ellison? At one point, during some poppyc…that is, some reference to sin or some-such, she actually wept. Most fascinating!'

Shaw frowned, and got the distinct feeling that that mystery of mysteries, that momentary sharing in the divine nature known as Holy Communion, had been looked upon by Landis in the same way he might regard the behaviour of rats in a laboratory cage.

'Come along,' said Landis with something approaching friendliness. 'Why don't you stay to luncheon?'

Shaw agreed, and contrary to his expectations, the meal was rather good, reminding him of the type of plain solid food he had eaten at his public school. Landis sat at the head of a long table, and held forth to Shaw on a number of subjects, mostly intended, thought Shaw, for self-glorification. Reeves was silent, looking carefully at the row of patients and scolding any that dropped food or appeared hesitant to eat.

Afterwards, as the patients shuffled back into the drawing room, he packed away his communion items and prepared to leave.

He felt a hand tug at his sleeve. It was Ruth.

Her eyes darted around the room, and Shaw noticed that the orderlies were looking elsewhere.

'He didn't die of a heart attack,' she whispered quickly. 'That man. Commander something.'

Shaw carried on packing his items and did not look up, but spoke quietly through a fixed smile.

'What happened?'

'They took him downstairs and…thank…than'you for'service. Ver'good…'

Puzzled by her change in tone, Shaw looked up and saw Reeves standing over Ruth.

'She's improving,' she snapped. 'She could barely speak a word until a week ago. Dr Landis really is a miracle worker.'

'Perhaps…' said Shaw. 'Might I have a little chat with…'

'I think the patients have had enough for today, Mr Shaw,' said Landis, who, Shaw noticed, had a habit of popping up when one least expected it. 'I expect you have other things to attend to. I shall see you to the gate.'

When he arrived home that afternoon, Shaw took out his communion items and cleaned them, packing them away neatly for the next week's service. He then frowned, realising something was missing from the little set.

His box of matches.

'The burden of them is intolerable...' Ruth thought back to the words of the communion service as she sat in the drawing room after Shaw had left. The familiar liturgy had begun to act upon her memory like oil on a stuck lock, and she fancied she could almost smell the little village church she had attended as a child. The bread and wine had seemed to act as a sort of spiritual stimulant beyond all rational explanation. *'To drink His blood that our sinful bodies may be made clean by His body...'* At that moment she had felt the fog in her mind began to clear as if it had been cut through by radiant sunshine.

She remembered what she had been trying so hard to remember. It was Eleanor! Her friend had been here, trapped in this place also, but had gone. Where had she gone? Had they...had she been taken down into the basement by those men, and...or had she somehow escaped?

To escape would have been so like Eleanor, she thought. They had been friends since the first term at boarding school. She had always been the stronger one, standing up to those filthy little *nouveaux-riches* snobs and bullies who thought it was their right to torment anybody that was different to them, especially somebody like Eleanor who had a title but no real money. Then her heart sank. No, it was too much to hope for. Nobody could escape from a place like this. And then she remembered something else. Why she had been brought here. And she wept.

Some time later, she woke with a start; she must have fallen asleep after the emotional release of her tears. The drawing room was empty, and it was dark outside; she realised it must soon be time for Reeves to come and give her her pills and then it would be time for bed. She was usually left until last as, she suspected, the other patients took longer to put to sleep.

She now felt completely lucid, and wondered if all traces of the horrible drugs they had filled her with had dissipated. It certainly felt like it. Now she could form a plan of action, as Eleanor would have done.

Once again she moved cautiously to the door and opened it a crack; the hallway was deserted. She could see Barton seated at the reception desk, reading a tabloid newspaper while moving his lips slightly. He took a packet of cigarettes from his tunic pocket and shook it when he found that it was empty. Then he stood up and walked up the stairs, presumably to his bedroom.

This was her chance! Ruth knew what was kept on that desk because she had noticed it when they had first brought her in; it seemed that even long-forgotten small details about her surroundings were beginning to return to her memory.

Silently she crossed to the desk and looked behind it. Yes, there it was; a small notepad and the stub of an indelible pencil. There were no pens, perhaps because they might be used as makeshift weapons by the patients, but a pencil would do.

Then she heard the familiar loud tap of footsteps along the stone corridor. It must be Reeves with her tablets! She snatched the pencil and a sheet of notepaper and stuffed them into her dressing gown pocket. She had to get back to the drawing room, but there was no time. Then the door opposite to her, which led to

Landis' office, began to open.

Instinctively she ducked down behind the desk out of sight. She could instead have remained in sight and feigned confusion, perhaps, and that might have worked with Reeves, but she was not sure if she could fool Landis.

'Miss Reeves,' he called out, 'would you come here please?'

The rattle of the nurse's footsteps grew louder and then stopped.

'Yes doctor?'

'Where on earth is Barton?' asked Landis tetchily. 'He was supposed to be on duty at the desk.'

'I have no idea, doctor,' said the nurse frostily. 'The orderlies are Mr Chivers' responsibility, not mine. Was there anything else? Only I have to give Miss Leigh-Ellison her medication.'

'And where is she?' asked Landis.

Ruth listened intently, and then heard a door opening upstairs and slow, ponderous footsteps at the end of the long linoleum-covered corridor that led to the staff bedrooms. She realised it must be Barton on his way back.

'I last saw her in the drawing room,' said Reeves. 'If you will excuse me, I will go.'

'Just one moment,' said Landis. 'I have something in mind for that young lady. Since I noticed her reaction to that clergyman's little performance, she has become of more interest to me.'

Ruth's eyes widened, and she listened in horror as Barton's footsteps reached the end of the corridor at the top of the stairs. He would be down any minute, and she would be found – but she must hear what Landis was going to say!

'I had originally scheduled Mrs Dalby for Wednesday evening, but I have changed my mind. Instead, I shall instruct the orderlies to take Miss Leigh-Ellison instead.'

Ruth heard the footsteps stop at the top of the stairs. Why didn't the great ox come down them, thought Ruth. Then it struck her – of course, he had heard the voices downstairs and realised he might be spotted away from his post. He was, she assumed, waiting until the coast was clear before returning.

'You mean take her to...' began Reeves.

'Yes, Miss Reeves,' said Landis. 'She is to be taken to the cellar, for treatment.'

'Very good, doctor.'

'In preparation for that she will require an increased dose of medication. Kindly come into my office to fetch it now.'

Ruth heard the doctor's door slam shut, and, with her legs trembling with fear, she darted out from behind the desk before Barton could notice her, and returned to her chair in the drawing room before Reeves arrived with her tablets.

She breathed in deeply, and fingered the pencil and paper in her pocket. The cellar, for 'treatment,' on Wednesday evening. She somehow knew that once she went into that cellar, she would not get out of it alive. The vicar was coming on Wednesday again, which meant he was her only hope.

Chapter Six

Major Wheatley put down the telephone and sighed. He had been hoping for a quiet afternoon in which he could do some digging about Ravenswood, but he had been summoned to his superior's office and 'F', as he pompously insisted on being called, was not the sort of man who liked to be kept waiting.

Wheatley put his jacket on and straightened his tie, then began the long walk along the linoleum-covered corridor with its green-painted walls and frosted glass partitions, from behind which came the clatter of typewriters and the ringing of many telephone bells.

Nodding to a man in naval uniform who passed him by, he knocked on a heavy wooden panelled door (no frosted glass for 'F'), and entered.

'His nibs in?' he asked the pretty young secretary in the outer office, who gave him a withering look and replied in an aristocratic drawl, 'If you mean Colonel Fellowes, then yes. Please take a seat and wait, Major.'

Wheatley sat down on a plush upright chair and examined his fingernails. He made no secret of his dislike of Colonel Fellowes, and the feeling was reciprocated. Wheatley was almost ten years his senior, and by rights, thought the Major, it should be him sitting in that office running the department and not some tyke who had got there through knowing the right people and going to the right school.

It particularly grated on Wheatley that the man had been commissioned after him, and had only seen service in the last six months of the war, and yet had managed to rise, seemingly effortlessly, to the rank of colonel. He had then secured a safe desk job which did not require any field work and always provided him with sufficient free time to attend country house parties and all the rest of it at weekends.

An intercom buzzed and the smart young secretary opened the green baize door on the other side of the room. Wheatley smiled and looked at her admiringly, but her face remained expressionless.

He shrugged and walked into the inner room, which was decorated more in the style of a duke's library than the office of a government functionary.

A tall, fine featured man with fair hair a little too long wearing a morning coat a little too perfectly tailored, faced him from behind a large antique desk.

'Ah, Wheatley, glad you could make it. Sit down.'

'Thank you sir,' said Wheatley, and plonked himself down in a chair opposite the Colonel, taking a packet of cigarettes out of his pocket.

'I'd rather you didn't smoke,' said Fellowes. 'I'll get to the point. What's this I hear about you poking around that hospital in Suffolk?'

'Ravenswood? I've given you an interim report on that, sir.'

'Yes, I read it, but I can't say I like it.'

'Anything in particular you object to, sir?'

'You should have had clearance from me before acting. This clergyman you've roped in, for one thing.'

'Mr Shaw? He's been of assistance previously and in my report I recommended he might be useful in…'

'Yes, I read all that,' said Fellowes with a dismissive wave of his hand. 'But what have you got him doing at this Ravenswood place?'

'He's taken a job as Chaplain, to act as my eyes and ears on the inside. I have reason to believe that there might be something…untoward…going on there, sir.'

'Untoward? Then why not get the police or the, the country medical board or whatever it is, to investigate?'

'We've tried, sir, but we've come up against opposition. In short, I think something's going on there that certain parties don't want me to know about, and I don't like it.'

Fellowes stood up and crossed to a drinks cabinet in the corner. He poured himself a glass of whisky but did not offer one to Wheatley.

'In that, Major, you are correct,' he said, returning to the desk. 'I shall stop stringing you along. One of the "certain parties" is me.'

'I don't follow, sir.'

'No, I didn't expect you would. Let me explain. Julian Landis has been the subject of a top secret investigation known about only by myself, the Home Secretary and two others at senior military staff level. Your blundering about and sending in this ridiculous parson may be about to jeopardise months of work.'

Wheatley gaped, and quickly shut his mouth. The little sneaking so-and-so!

'May I ask what the investigation has…'

'No you may not,' snapped Fellowes. 'If you had approached me first…'

'You would have blocked me as well,' interrupted Wheatley.

'Do not interrupt me,' said Fellowes, raising his voice slightly. 'Quite frankly I don't like your manner.'

Wheatley felt his hackles rise. 'Bill Raikes never had cause for complaint about my manner, sir, and he was head of this department for a good few years more than you.'

'Colonel Raikes has been retired for nearly two years, Wheatley,' said Fellowes, his voice quivering with suppressed anger. 'And it has taken me most of that time to sort out the mess he left.'

'Mess?' asked Wheatley incredulously.

'Yes!' said Fellowes, banging his whisky glass down on the desk. 'Raikes set this department up at the end of the war, when things were done a damned sight differently than they are now. Back then one could get away with running an operation with a bunch of misfits, insubordinates and glasshouse-dodgers led by... *temporary gentlemen!*'

The last epithet, felt Wheatley, was clearly aimed at him, and he felt a sudden desire to punch Fellowes on the nose. Instead, he took a deep breath and smiled.

'I'm quite aware my chaps and I are not your sort, sir,' he replied sweetly. 'Remind me of where you saw service in the war again. Somewhere on the Isle of Wight, if I recall?'

Fellowes appeared not to hear the remark and stared blankly ahead. 'I've got him,' thought Wheatley. 'He can't answer that one as he knows quite well the only thing he's ever shot dead is a pheasant.'

'I've no time to bandy words, Wheatley,' said

Fellowes after a pause. 'What is important is what we do now. It's possible we *might* be able to salvage something from this fiasco. Has this Reverend Shaw reported to you yet?'

'Not yet, sir.'

'Very well. When he does, I want to know everything he finds out. But he is absolutely not to do anything which might lead to his exposure. Is that clear?'

'Mr Shaw's a reliable man, sir. Ex-forces himself, in the chaplaincy. He won't let me down. It would help though if you give me – and him – some idea of what we're looking for.'

Colonel Fellowes sighed, and drained the last of the whisky in his glass.

'We've been keeping an eye on Landis because word's got out that he's developed a new form of treatment for mental conditions. Ever seen shell-shock?'

'Of course.'

'That's how we found out about him. He treated…let's just call him someone high up in the general staff…who'd been suffering from it on and off for years. Worked wonders, apparently. Some sort of pill, or injection, that calms them down and helps them get back to normal. This patient spoke to someone in the Admiralty who then spoke to me. But Landis didn't seem to want anyone to know about it, and when he was approached he point blank refused to give away the details. That's when we started to get suspicious.'

'What about the deaths?' asked Wheatley.

'Deaths?'

'At least three patients at Ravenswood in the last two years. Heart failure, apparently. But try talking to the coroner about it and see where you get.'

'The coroner has been instructed to look the other way,' said Fellowes. 'And the police. Which is why you came up against a brick wall.'

'But...why, sir?' asked Wheatley. 'If he's killing his patients...'

'We have no evidence of that,' insisted Fellowes. 'It's possible the deaths were coincidences, or unfortunate accidents. We are not about to risk Landis' work by having some flat-footed regional copper or tuppenny-ha'penny county coroner charging around Ravenswood like a bull in a china shop. And certainly not some clergyman who dabbles in private detection in his spare time!'

'But how would that risk Landis' work...?'

Fellowes sighed. 'Have you any idea how important to the national interest it would be to successfully treat lunacy? Particularly shell-shock. When the next war comes – and it's coming, mark my words, you've seen the reports on German re-armament – it will give us a huge advantage over the enemy. We'll be able to send shell-shocked men back into action in days. And as for civilians, when the bombing raids start, there could be mass psychosis. If Landis' treatment really works... '

'You'll have a nation of good little zombies,' said Wheatley dryly. 'And you can't risk a public investigation into his methods because the Germans – or the Russians, God help us – will start getting interested. And they'll either steal his ideas, or steal *him*.'

'I think you're getting the picture.'

'Not entirely, sir. If this Landis doesn't want to work

for us, I don't see how…'

'You are sometimes rather more naive than one might expect, given your record,' said Fellowes. 'If Landis won't willingly serve his king and country by agreeing to work with us, then by God he'll be made to do so *un*willingly.'

Wheatley frowned. He realised he had come a very long way from that August day in 1914 when he had eagerly queued at the recruitment office to defend 'plucky little Belgium'.

'I see,' said Wheatley. 'You want me to find something on him, and use it against him so he co-operates.'

'Precisely,' said Fellowes. 'If those patients died because of some sort of unorthodox medical intervention, then Landis could spend the rest of his life behind bars if we choose to stop protecting him.'

'But if he works for us he gets off scot-free.'

'More or less. Do you think your parson can get the proof we need?'

'I think so. He's cracked several murder cases that had the police baffled, and I don't know any other man I could get into the place without suspicion. But I'll need to brief him on what he's looking for.'

'Then do so, Major. But only give him the minimum information required to do the job. And if he gets into trouble, he's on his own. Do I make myself clear?'

'As crystal, sir.'

Shaw had just returned from weekday morning prayer (attended, as usual, by only the verger and the warden and himself) and was trying to coax the first pipe of the day into life, when he heard the telephone bell ringing. Moments later, Hettie entered his study to inform him that a London caller was on the line.

'I thought you did not trust the telephone,' said Shaw when he realised who was calling.

'I don't,' said Wheatley, 'but it's faster than letters and I haven't got time to motor down to Suffolk for another round of golf, more's the pity. I'll be brief. Have you anything to report?'

Once Shaw had established that Hettie was out of earshot (she was upstairs helping Mrs Shaw to air the beds), he told Wheatley about the incident with Ruth after Holy Communion.

'Did she say how she knew this man Commander Elphick had been killed?' asked the Major.

'There was no time,' said Shaw. 'All she related was that they took him downstairs. I assume that is to the cellar – when I expressed interest in the door leading to it, Landis was evasive. Everyone is watched in that place, which is suspicious in itself. Of course, it may ostensibly be to prevent the patients coming to harm, but it seems more than that. The nurse, Reeves, is particularly observant. I think she suspected something, which is why Miss Leigh-Ellison had to break off our conversation.'

'I see,' said Wheatley slowly. 'If Elphick was a Commander there'll be something on him at the Admiralty so I'll see what I can find. Keep at it, Mr Shaw. Try to isolate this woman and get some more information out of her.' He chuckled. 'It's a pity your lot don't go in for confessions as that would be the perfect excuse to get her somewhere undisturbed.'

'Have you managed to uncover anything at your end?' enquired Shaw. 'It would help if I had some idea of what I was looking for. At present it is like looking for a needle in a haystack whilst not even knowing what a needle looks like.'

There was a pause, and Shaw wondered if they had been disconnected.

'Are you still there, Major Wheatley?' he asked.

'I'm here. Look, it's a bit more complicated than I first thought. I've done a bit of digging at this end and it looks like Landis is involved in some sort of experimental treatment for mental disorders. But what we don't know is why he's being so hush-hush about it. Have you seen any evidence of that?'

'I suggested to Landis that some sort of medical process was being used on the patients,' said Shaw, 'and he agreed, but he would reveal nothing more than that. He did indeed seem rather evasive.'

'Hmm, that's interesting,' said Wheatley. 'Now it's my guess this treatment he's using is unorthodox and it's resulting in the deaths of patients, which is why he's being cagey about it. Now if you can get firm evidence of that, we can then…'

There was another pause. Shaw heard the crackle of static on the long-distance line, and then a long sigh.

'I'm still here,' said Wheatley. 'Once you get the evidence we can deal with the matter. Keep me posted. I'll let you go now as I daresay you've got brasses to rub or something.'

Shaw ended the conversation and returned to his study. He absent-mindedly stuffed his pipe with tobacco until he realised it was over-full, and he had to empty it and start all over again. Of course, it was hard to tell over the telephone, but he could not help feeling Wheatley was hiding something from him.

Just as he had sat down and picked up his sermon notes for the following Sunday, the telephone rang again and he made it to the instrument before Hettie could arrive.

'Carry on upstairs, please, Hettie,' he said to the servant as she stood at the top of the stairs. She gave him a quizzical glance then disappeared.

'Addenham 324,' he said into the mouthpiece, and there was the sound of the A button being pressed and coins dropping into a call-box.

'Is that Reverend Shaw?'

The voice was familiar.

'Speaking. May I assume this is…'

'Please don't say my name,' said the woman. 'I think you know who I am. Can you meet me in your church in ten minutes?'

'Certainly,' said Shaw. 'But what…'

The line went dead.

Ten minutes later Shaw entered his nearby church to see a woman kneeling in one of the pews at the back of the church. She wore an expensive looking felt hat and a tweed suit with a fox-fur wrap; every inch of her oozed wealth and good taste. She looked younger, Shaw thought, than she sounded on the telephone, which tended to impart age to the voice.

Shaw coughed discretely and the woman opened her

eyes and stood up. She looked around the church and, presumably once satisfied it was empty, she approached Shaw and held out a gloved hand.

'I'm sorry to have to be so furtive, Mr Shaw,' she said. 'My husband believes I am visiting a distant cousin, which I shall do later, and my driver has been left to take refreshment at your village teashop, in the belief that I am exploring a beautiful village church discovered entirely by chance.'

'Why are you here, Lady Stoneleigh?'

'I was praying for the repose of Eleanor's soul. I know that isn't entirely approved of in the good old C of E, but it seems to have become more common since the war. What is your opinion?'

'The objections by the reformers to prayers for the dead,' said Shaw, 'were, I believe, largely because they were abused by the unscrupulous in order to make money.'

'Ah yes,' said Lady Stoneleigh. 'The medieval rich could afford to pay people to pray for their souls in perpetuity, whereas the poor had to simply hope their surviving relations would oblige them free of charge.'

'Something like that,' said Shaw. 'But I do not think you came here to discuss theology. Shall we go into the vestry?'

Shaw led the way into the little shadowy room to the right of the east window, and closed the door behind them.

He offered Lady Stoneleigh the only chair in the room, behind a battered Gothic Revival desk.

'I tried to put all this out of my mind,' she said, 'but then I realised that was the coward's way out. And now that my daughter is dead, I have come to feel as if I no longer care if I live or die. Does that shock you?'

'It is a more common reaction in the bereaved than you might think,' said Shaw. 'But you have two sons, and a husband. Think of your duty to them.'

'Yes of course,' said Lady Stoneleigh. 'Don't worry, I'm not about to hurl myself off a bridge or take arsenic. What I mean is, the thought of dying no longer worries me.'

'At the risk of speaking in platitudes, it should not worry any person of faith,' said Shaw carefully. 'But why should the matter arise? Are you ill?'

'Ill? Certainly not.' Lady Stoneleigh laughed and he suddenly saw how closely she resembled her late daughter. 'My people have the constitution of oxes. We go on into our nineties, causing the most frightful impatience in our heirs. No, what I mean is, Mr Shaw, I think when I have told you what I am going to say, it is quite possible that someone will have me killed.'

'Go on,' said Shaw, without missing a beat.

'You do not seem surprised,' said Lady Stoneleigh.

'When one has been a clergyman as long as I,' said Shaw, 'one is painfully aware that the depths to which sinful man can descend are far deeper than can ever be sounded. Nothing would surprise me now, I fear.'

'Very well,' said Lady Stoneleigh, and the little tenor bell in the church clock tower struck the hour. She looked at her watch and then at Shaw.

'I shall be brief. I agree with your supposition that my daughter was murdered. And one thing I am certain of is that she was *not* mad.'

'From what I saw of her briefly, I should say the

same,' said Shaw. He quickly explained what had happened on the night when Eleanor had arrived at Keating's house.

'My people, and my husband's,' said Lady Stoneleigh, 'have family trees several feet long. There has never been a hint of insanity in either of them. Eleanor was always an entirely reasonable and balanced girl, in particular contrast, I may add, to the lax standards of many of her generation.

'She did not overly indulge in alcohol nor was she interested in night-clubs or dance-bands and I am quite certain she would not take the illicit drugs one reads about in the newspapers.

'Our only concern was that she did not seem able to find a man she liked well enough to marry, but I think that was more a sign of her good sense than anything else. Many young men seem to lack character these days.'

'Very well,' said Shaw. 'She was not mad. But how do you know she was murdered?'

'I do not,' said Lady Stoneleigh. 'But I sense it. And I would like to know on what you base your conviction of it.'

Shaw explained about the cleaner at Liverpool Street Station and his witnessing of Eleanor being pushed under a train. Lady Stoneleigh nodded throughout, and did not display the slightest hint of emotion.

'The description fits,' she said. 'The thug who pushed Eleanor is presumably the same one who visited us in London. He was with a smaller man, of the…how can one put it…of the type one imagines sells second hand motor cars in Great Portland Street.'

'Chivers,' said Shaw with distaste. 'He is the head orderly at Ravenswood, the place in which I believe your daughter was incarcerated. The other one is Barton, his lackey. But why did they visit *you*?'

'They said that they represented a private hospital. We were not told where, simply that Eleanor had been taken there after an...episode. We were not permitted to visit her. They said she had had some sort of fit in the street. The police and a doctor had to be summoned. But it was a lie, a lie I tell you!'

For the first time Shaw noticed that Lady Stoneleigh was wringing her gloved hands tightly, and he put a reassuring hand on her shoulder.

'You believe it was...induced in some way?'

'Precisely. At first I thought it was all made up, but there were police reports and committal papers and...oh, it was so degrading...but I *knew* it was deliberate. My daughter was drugged or poisoned in some way, she simply must have been. And when we tried to find out what had happened, the police refused to help us.

'That man, Chivers, called again a few days later, and told us in no uncertain terms that unless we stopped pursuing the matter, Eleanor's life would be in danger. We were told to forget all about the matter until she was well enough to return home. At that point I somehow *knew* she was never going to come back.

'He also made it clear something awful might happen to our boys if we spoke to anyone. That's why my husband treated you so abominably when you called. He was terrified you were some sort of journalist and it was all going to be exposed, putting their lives in danger.'

'I see,' replied Shaw. 'But why would they do this to Eleanor?'

Lady Stoneleigh took a deep breath and regained her composure.

'It was because she had threatened to talk to the newspapers. About Ruth.'

Ruth's mood over the next few days swung between despair and hope. She continued to spit out her medication without Reeves noticing, and now she remembered. She remembered everything. And she knew why she was being kept in Ravenswood.

She had also become lucid enough to realise the full horror of her situation. Before she had stopped swallowing the pills, nothing seemed to matter. She had spent her days in a cloud of unknowing; a warm bath of mental torpor in which nothing seemed to matter, and in which there was neither past nor future. But now, she had to face things as they really were.

It was no good giving into despair, she thought. What was done was done. And she had, at least, a slim chance of escape. If only she could get word to Reverend Shaw! If that did not work, there was only one other course open to her, and she hardly dared think about *that*.

It was the morning, and she was lying in bed waiting the arrival of Reeves and her morning pill. She would then, as usual, be escorted to the bathroom. At least they trusted her that much, she thought. The idea of Reeves, or worse, one of the orderlies, watching her while she bathed filled her with horror. Then breakfast would be served and the long, tedious day would begin as so many others had.

It had only been bearable because her brain had been addled by Landis' medication, she saw that now. And now that she could think clearly again, she realised the full horror of her situation. She could not reason with Landis, because it would then become clear to him that she had stopped taking the pills. She wondered if he would soon notice the deception anyway, perhaps with some sort of blood test or simply by examining her.

Escape, then, she decided, was her only hope. And she was on her own. The other patients, poor things, were too far gone to be of any help to her. The one good thing about the place was that Landis seemed to place a great deal of confidence in the pills he had forced down the patients' throats.

He must assume, she realised, that everyone was too heavily doped to attempt escape. This was why, she guessed, they trusted her to be left alone much of the time and gave her a certain amount of free movement, rather than keeping her locked up all the time, at least in the day. It was her only advantage, and she had to preserve it for as long as possible.

She remembered that Reverend Shaw would be coming again in two days. Two days! It seemed an age away. She crossed from her bed over to the wall, where a hot-water radiator was concealed behind a metal grille. For obvious reasons, open fires were not permitted in the bedrooms. She poked her little finger into one of the holes in the grille, near the bottom, and was reassured to feel the slip of paper wrapped tightly around the stub of indelible pencil that she had taken from the front desk. Nobody had found it.

Emboldened by the success of her theft, she resolved that she would do a bit more exploring and see if she could find any other useful items that might help her in a breakout. Then she heard footsteps on the corridor outside – the familiar tattoo of the metal segments on Reeves' nasty cheap shoes. She jumped back into the bed and pretended to be asleep.

After Lady Stoneleigh had left, Shaw sat in his church for a while, alternating between prayer and deep thought. What he had been told had unsettled him, and he was not quite certain of how to proceed. Who was it, he wondered, who had really ordered Lord and Lady Stoneleigh to keep quiet about their daughter's incarceration? Ostensibly it had come from Chivers, but Shaw could hardly imagine it was his idea. He must have been given orders. From Landis, presumably. But was there anyone above Landis?

He returned to the vicarage and, once he had made sure that his wife and servant were out of earshot, he telephoned Wheatley.

'I hope you're keeping a record of these calls,' said the Major. 'You can claim the cost back if you time them. Form G12, the one I gave you.'

'Thank you Major, but I have something more pressing on my mind at present. Something I think you should know.'

'Go on.'

Shaw took a deep breath.

'I had a visit today from Baroness Stoneleigh. '

'Who's she when she's at home?'

'The mother of the late Honourable Eleanor Harrington.'

'Ah.'

'She believes that her daughter was incarcerated at Ravenswood under false pretences. When she and her husband tried to look into the matter, threats were made. I don't think I need to spell them out.'

'Who threatened them?'

'Chivers, the orderly, and his accomplice. But I expect the idea came from someone else.'

'I see. So why did she risk speaking to you?'

'Because, Major, she is an extremely brave woman.'

'I'll take your word for that. But why lock up Eleanor?'

'Like her mother, she was a forthright and confident woman. And she threatened to expose Landis.'

'What did she have on him?'

'According to Lady Stoneleigh, Eleanor had a friend. A close friend from her school-days, called Ruth Leigh-Ellison. Miss Leigh-Ellison was...was deceived by a much older married man.'

'You're not talking to the Mother's Union now, Mr Shaw. You mean she was knock, er, she was got into trouble by this fellow?'

'That is correct. He refused to have anything to do with her. She threatened to expose him, and he met that with a counter-threat that her life, and that of the child, would be endangered if she continued with such threats. She complied, and was sent away to the country.

'This man was no ordinary man. I do not know his name, and nor does anyone else, it seems, but he was of a high social standing. Extremely high, and the revelation that he had fathered a child outside wedlock would have ruined him.

'I am sorry to say the child died at a few days old. Following this, Miss Leigh-Ellison felt she had nothing to lose and again threatened to expose the man. It was after that that she suddenly had some sort of unexpected attack of insanity, and was taken away.'

'Let me guess,' said Wheatley. 'She was taken to Ravenswood.'

'Correct. But not before she had told everything to her best friend, Eleanor Harrington, who also confided in her mother, Lady Stoneleigh.'

'What about Ruth's parents?'

'They refused to discuss the matter with Eleanor. She assumed they too had been threatened and were too frightened to talk to her.'

'Any history of insanity in Ruth's family? Or Eleanor's, come to that?'

'No. Both seemed remarkably level-headed young women.'

'Hmm. What if Landis somehow knew this…man… and they hatched a plan to declare Ruth mad and have her locked up? Then when Eleanor found out about it he did the same to her.'

'Perhaps. It sounds…'

'It sounds like the sort of nonsense my wife's always dragging me off to see at the cinema. Next you'll be telling me Landis tied one of them to a railway track.'

'I can see no other explanation,' said Shaw. 'One of them going insane, perhaps, but *both* young women, given what they knew?'

'I had a nose around the Admiralty the other day,' said Wheatley, 'about this Commander Elphick that died in Ravenswood. Now he went doolally all right, but there was nothing in his record about a dicky ticker.'

'A dicky...'

'Ticker. Heart. You said Landis said he died of a heart attack. Sound as a bell, according to his doctor's report at discharge. But when I tried to find out how he got into Ravenswood, another brick wall came up.'

'What do you think it all means, Major Wheatley?'

'I think Landis might have started out as a genuine doctor, but something's changed along the way. I think not only is he doing things to people he oughtn't, but he's taken on a new type of work. That of keeping people out of the way that the great and good don't want known about.'

'But that is preposterous. Surely such things do not happen?'

'Oh, they happen Mr Shaw. We know the Soviets have been locking up anyone they don't like in asylums for a few years now. But they can do what they like and nobody can complain. Here though, well, we've got things like *habeas corpus* and a free press, and you can't get away with that sort of thing so easily.'

'But one might, if one was able to simulate the *symptoms* of madness,' said Shaw slowly.

'Exactly,' said Wheatley. 'But it can't be working that

well, because otherwise Landis wouldn't have to resort to making death threats to anyone who looked too closely into what he was doing. I reckon he can fool the average copper and magistrate and perhaps a family doctor enough to get people locked away, but if an expert head-doctor was involved he'd be found out'

'Then I must find evidence of this,' said Shaw decisively. 'As soon as possible.'

'Yes, Mr Shaw. But it's clear to me now this Landis is a highly dangerous man – and he's protected. Know how to use a revolver?'

Shaw thought of the last time he had tried to use such a weapon – on the roof of Midchester Cathedral when faced with a determined killer. He had failed to use it properly, resulting in the man being maimed for life. He shook his head sadly.

'If you are proposing I should carry a gun while administering Holy Communion, the answer is no. I have "put on the full armour of God" and that will be sufficient protection.'

'All right, all right,' placated Wheatley. 'I just hope that can stop a knife or a bullet. And I'll say it again. For God's sake be careful. The moment you think they might have rumbled you, *get out of there.*'

Chapter Seven

The following Wednesday, Ruth got out of bed early and extricated the pencil and paper from behind the radiator grille. She had not risked writing anything until now, in case it were found, but she had thought for a long time about what she would write, and now neatly printed it in large block capitals. She placed the note in her dressing gown pocket and returned the pencil to its hiding place in case it should be needed again.

That, however, she thought, was unlikely. If this attempt to get a message to Reverend Shaw did not work, there would not be a chance for another. She shuddered at the thought of what might happen in the basement, and put the thought out of her head. There was no point dwelling on it. The note *must* work.

Soon she heard the familiar footsteps of Reeves in the corridor, and the turning of the key in the lock. Reeves was her usual icy self, making polite conversation but with no real warmth behind it. How, thought Ruth, was the woman able to work in a place like this, day in, day out? She must be utterly amoral, devoid of all human compassion.

'Dr Landis has instructed you will be on double the usual dose for the foreseeable future,' she said. 'He is concerned about your progress.'

'Not slow enough?' Ruth nearly blurted out, but then

realised she must keep up the act of appearing insane for as long as possible. She gazed ahead blankly and took the pills, then pretended to swallow them.

'Down the hatch,' chirped Reeves. Ruth took a sip of the offered water, and allowed some of it to dribble down her chin in the hope of appearing 'in character' as a lunatic.

'Messy girl,' chided Reeves. 'Where's your hankie? You've usually one in your dressing gown pocket.'

'Don't have one.'

In the effort to talk whilst keeping the pills hidden under her tongue, Ruth dribbled far more than she had intended to and Reeves flashed her a hostile glance.

'Don't be silly. I can't have Barton taking you to the bathroom looking like that. Where is your handkerchief?'

Reeves reached out to put her hand in Ruth's pocket. Ruth pushed the hand away, and cried 'no!'

'What on earth is the matter?' said Reeves angrily. 'What have you got in...'

Ruth felt her whole body slump with a sensation of despair as Reeves pulled the note out of her pocket. The pills were dissolving under her tongue, and she forced herself not to swallow in case any of the filthy poison should go down her throat.

Reeves looked at the note and her eyes widened in surprise. She read it out slowly. 'Reverend Shaw. Please help kept prisoner against will. Not mad. Forceably medicated. Get me out. No police. R. Leigh-Ellison.'

Reeves inhaled deeply. 'You wicked, deceitful girl,' she hissed. 'After all Dr Landis has done for you. After all *I* have done for you. What have you to say for yourself?'

Ruth did not dare open her mouth and merely shook her head.

'Speak up!' barked Reeves. When Ruth refused, a knowing look crossed the nurse's face.

'You haven't been swallowing those pills, have you?' she asked. 'Open your mouth now.'

Ruth shook her head again.

'Open your mouth now, you stupid girl, or I shall send for Barton. I'm sure he'll relish the job of doing it forceably.'

Ruth opened her mouth wide, allowing Reeves to see the pills.

'I thought as much,' said Reeves. 'I thought I could trust you to behave sensibly, but it seems I cannot. Spit them out. No, not on the floor, into the commode. That's it. Dr Landis says they do not work properly if they are allowed to dissolve inside the mouth. Now I shall have to go to his office and get more. A fine morning this has turned out to be, with extra work such as that when I have others to attend to.'

Ruth looked mutely at her, tears welling in her eyes, but she choked them back. She did not want to give this harridan the satisfaction of knowing what torment she was in.

'And as for this,' said Reeves, holding up the note, 'I shall have to think about what to do. Where did you get pencil and paper?'

Ruth remained silent.

'I see – refusing to answer. My guess is you stole them from the reception desk. I have warned Barton about leaving items there before. He has even left the keys to the front door there on more than one occasion. Where have you hidden the pencil?'

Ruth shook her head.

'Never mind,' snapped Reeves. 'I shall have this room searched from top to bottom. My first instinct is to inform Dr Landis and have you confined to your room indefinitely, but I am not a hard woman. Up until now you have been a model patient so I am tempted to overlook it. But you must not make any further attempt at passing notes. What on earth did you think you would achieve by it? Why would Mr Shaw believe you? He would most likely have reported you immediately to Dr Landis.'

Ruth remained silent and glared at the nurse.

'Very well,' sighed Reeves. 'I do not have time to go down to fetch more medication before breakfast is served. You shall have to go without today. But don't blame me if you feel the worse for it.'

Reeves stomped out of the room and the heavy door clanged shut. Once she was sure the woman was out of earshot, Ruth threw herself down on her bed and began to sob.

Before setting up his temporary altar in the drawing room at Ravenswood, Shaw asked to see Landis, and was invited into his office.

'A glass of sherry, Mr Shaw?' asked the doctor.

'Thank you but no. I wanted to speak to you about private confession.'

'I don't quite follow. Are you suggesting that I have something to confess?'

'No, no,' said Shaw. 'I mean your patients. Residents, that is. You see, I was talking to an, an acquaintance recently and the subject of confession came up. I wondered if you might allow your patients to be offered that.'

'Forgive me Mr Shaw. I have not the slightest interest in church matters as you know, but I was under the impression it was the Roman Catholics who practiced confession. You are an Anglican.'

'Indeed. And you are correct in that our Roman Catholic brethren are the ones who practice confession as a necessary prelude to taking Holy Communion. But in the Anglican tradition it is also recommended that any person in contention with his or her neighbour ought to confess the matter before taking Communion. The Prayer Book makes that quite clear. In fact I can show you the relevant passage.'

Shaw took out his pocket prayer book but Landis waved it away with a bored gesture. 'I really do not have the time for this sort of thing,' he drawled. 'But the overseers in their wisdom require it so I have little choice but to comply. What is it you are asking of me?'

'Merely that I should be allowed to speak to each patient briefly in private before the service, to give them the opportunity to unburden themselves if they so require it. In their bedrooms, perhaps.'

'Mr Shaw, my patients, as you know, are barely cognisant of what is going on around them. I doubt they can remember much beyond what they ate for breakfast. They are hardly likely to be wracked with guilt over past offences. Besides, Miss Leigh-Ellison was the only person to take communion when you were here last week.'

'The reticence of the others to come forward may be because of the reasons I have just stated,' said Shaw.

Shaw held his breath. He was gambling on the fact that Landis, being antithetical to religion, would not know that confessional interviews before communion were hardly ever practised nowadays. It was indeed mentioned in the Prayer Book, but he could not ever recall it being carried out.

'Very well,' said Landis. 'Do what you must. But I doubt you will hear anything of any coherence except perhaps from Miss Leigh-Ellison. I shall have the orderlies escort the patients to their rooms now. But kindly come earlier next week so that you can speak to them before they leave their rooms. It takes a certain amount of effort to move these people around, as I am sure you can imagine.'

Shaw nodded, and breathed a small sigh of relief which he hoped the man could not hear. He reached into his pocket to assure himself that two certain items he had brought with him were still there, and walked to the drawing room.

After he had set out his communion table, Shaw looked up to see Chivers looking at him with a hostile smile. Behind him stood Barton and Gauge, looking at him blankly. They made Shaw think of the Easter Island statues he had once seen in a magic-lantern lecture.

Suddenly he realised where he had seen Barton before, and he almost started with shock. It had been in a pulpit! Yes, that was it – the man had not only been a boxer, but also a lay preacher for some nonconformist sect. 'Bible Basher Barton', the papers had called him. He had been something of a sensation five or six years previously. Shaw, out of curiosity, had gone to hear him preach at Midchester City Chapel, and recalled the crowds of boys with autograph books mobbing him at the end of the service.

He had preached competently, though not with any great intellectual insight, Shaw recalled. But he had had a charismatic aura about him that was completely gone now. How had it happened? The figure he saw before him now seemed a lumbering, amoral wreck of a man. No wonder he had not recognised him.

'They're all banged up again now vicar,' said Chivers, shaking Shaw out of his reverie.

'Banged…up?'

'Yus, that's what we used to call it in…well, it means they're all back in their rooms, like Dr Landis ordered. Miss Reeves will open them up for you, then we'll bring them back down for church parade.'

'Thank you. I shall begin my rounds.'

'Oh, and a word to the wise, eh, vicar,' said Chivers. 'Don't spring that on us again will you? It's a terrible palava getting them back in their rooms and out again. Some of them think it's bedtime already.'

'I agreed with Dr Landis,' said Shaw, 'that I should come earlier next week to speak to the patients before they are brought from their rooms in the morning.'

'You do that, vicar. Save us a lot of bother.'

The man continued to gaze at him with that curious hostile smile.

'Thank you, Chivers,' said Shaw, and walked towards

the drawing room door, and he felt three sets of eyes watching him intently as he did so.

Reeves met him on the stairs and together they walked up to the first floor, with its long institutional corridor smelling of polish and disinfectant. Shaw felt sorry for having to subject the patients to the inconvenience of being locked up in their rooms again, but it was the only way he could think of carrying out his plan undisturbed.

'I should like to see Miss Leigh-Ellison first,' said Shaw. 'Of all the patients she was the only one to take Holy Communion last week. Do you know much about her?'

'You cannot expect me to divulge personal information about patients,' said Reeves as she led Shaw briskly along the corridor. 'Here is her room. Please don't be too long as the orderlies will have a job getting everyone downstairs again. I fail to see why this could not have been done in the drawing room.'

'I daresay,' said Shaw, 'you would not particularly like to divulge your inmost thoughts to a clergyman whilst in the hearing of others, would you, Miss Reeves?'

'I wouldn't wish to do it even if it were in a sound-proofed room,' she snapped. 'My thoughts are my own, thank you. Five minutes.'

Reeves rattled the key in the lock and pushed the door open. 'The chaplain wants a word,' she said, 'so make sure you behave yourself.'

Shaw stepped into the room. Ruth was sitting on the bed, with a look of complete surprise on her face.

The door clanged shut behind them, and they were

alone. Shaw decided to risk using the items he had brought with him.

'Good morning, Miss Leigh-Ellison,' he said brightly, then pulled out a notepad from his pocket. He showed it to Ruth, and her eyes widened. Upon it he had written in large letters 'Do you need help? Please write quickly.'

Ruth nodded enthusiastically but then looked to the door and put a finger to her lips and then waggled her ear.

Thinking he understood her meaning, Shaw passed a pencil to Ruth and spoke loudly while she began to scribble.

'Shall I say the Lord's Prayer?' he asked.

'Yes please, chaplain,' she replied, while scribbling furiously on the pad.

Shaw closed his eyes and began to pray loudly, hoping that if somebody, presumably Reeves, were listening from behind the door, it would drown out the sound of the pencil scratching rapidly on the pad.

Shaw then took out his prayer book and began reciting one of the psalms. When he had finished, Ruth thrust the pad into his hand and sat back on the bed.

He looked quickly at the pad. In block capitals she had written:

I AM NOT MAD. KEPT HERE AGAINST WILL. IF YOU DON'T BELIEVE ME ASK LADY STONELEIGH C/O 15 BOURNE SQUARE LONDON SW. I MUST GET OUT BEFORE TONIGHT. LIFE IN DANGER.

Shaw took the pencil from Ruth and, while he intoned the twenty-third psalm from memory, he hurriedly scribbled beneath it:

WHAT WILL HAPPEN TONIGHT?

He passed the pad and pencil back, but before Ruth could write anything, he heard a rattle of keys in the lock. He had just enough time to snatch back the pad and pencil and conceal them in his jacket pocket before standing up.

'In the name of the Father and of the Son and of the Holy Spirit, amen,' he pronounced whilst making the sign of the cross over Ruth, who sat hunched forward with her eyes closed as if deep in prayer.

'Come along now please,' said Reeves as she bustled into the room.

'Thank you for allowing me to pray with you, Miss Leigh-Ellison,' said Shaw. 'I look forward to seeing you at Holy Communion shortly. Please remember that there is always hope, and that our deliverance may be closer at hand than we think.'

'What was she talking to you about?' asked Reeves suspiciously as she locked Ruth's door.

'My dear Miss Reeves,' said Shaw politely, 'you cannot expect me to divulge personal information about parishioners.'

'Oh very well,' said Reeves as she walked rapidly along the corridor. 'She is probably the most lucid of the patients so don't think you'll get a similar response from any of the others. This is all a waste of time, if you ask me. This is Miss Layton's room.'

Shaw realised sadly that the woman was right; the other four patients were barely aware of his presence and he prayed briefly and perfunctorily with them in turn, speaking like an automaton as he wracked his brains about what he should do.

He was still unsure as Reeves led him back down the corridor and he awaited the arrival of the patients in the drawing room.

Landis entered and sat on one of the upright chairs ranged along the side of the room, and then Barton, Gauge and Reeves led in the patients, as Chivers took up a defensive position by the French doors, looking at Shaw with that same hostile smile.

Then something happened. He was not sure what had caused it, as he had his back turned to the room while he put on his cassock. Just before he put on his surplice, he was shoved in the back and looked round to see one of the patients, Mr Grant, toppling forwards toward him with his arms outstretched.

'No!' slurred the man with a look of frozen horror in his eyes. Shaw wondered what tortured image the man was seeing, and held up his hands to support him, as he fell forward. Reeves, Barton and Chivers rushed to restrain the man, pulling him off Shaw. In the general melee, Shaw felt a sharp sensation in his leg, as if someone had shoved a hand into his trouser pocket. What on earth was happening?

After Mr Grant had been helped to a chair and calmed down, Shaw took a deep breath and began the communion service. Relieved that his cassock had a flap enabling him to reach into his trouser pocket, he removed his handkerchief and feigned blowing his nose, then replaced the handkerchief in his pocket. Before he withdrew his hand, he felt the presence of an object that had not been there before. It was the unmistakeable metal shape of a key.

Major Wheatley breathed in the fresh, damp air of St James' Park as he strolled through the lunch-time crowds, past little groups of clerks and secretaries on benches enjoying the mild weather, eating sandwiches out of greaseproof paper packets. Soon, he thought, it would be warm enough for a silver band to play on the bandstand and spring would be properly underway.

He was tempted to remove his mackintosh, but he hesitated when he remembered who he was walking with. Colonel Fellowes, he suspected, would probably think it was infra-dig to do such a thing. Then he chuckled to himself. As if he cared what the chinless wonder thought!

'Getting warm,' he murmured, and removed his coat, slinging it over his shoulder. He guessed Fellowes would probably think that a worse infringement of ettiquette than carrying it over his forearm, and to add to the gesture he also loosened his tie slightly.

'Fiddling studs,' he said to nobody in particular as he struggled to relieve the pressure on his neck from his shirt collar.

He smiled as he caught a withering glance from Fellowes, who looked down his nose at him and swiped at a weed on the path with his tightly furled umbrella.

'May I ask what you've brought me out here for sir?' asked Wheatley. 'I like a stroll in the park but I don't think you've brought me out here for my health.'

'Indeed not,' said Fellowes. 'Let us just say that "walls have ears", even in Whitehall.'

'*Particularly* in Whitehall, I should say,' said Wheatley. What on earth was the man on about, he thought. Was he going round the twist? It wasn't possible to do a job like theirs if you were always worried about people listening at keyholes. As long as you weren't too obvious, like writing postcards or getting tight and mouthing off in pubs, you would be all right. All this skulking around and playing at spies was making him feel uneasy.

Fellowes looked around him as if to admire the park, but Wheatley suspected he was making sure nobody was in earshot.

'What I am about to say may shock you,' he said.

'I highly doubt that, sir.'

'Very well. It's about your clergyman friend, Mr Shaw.'

Wheatley paused before speaking.

'No objections to a smoke out here, sir?'

Fellowes ignored the question and watched with distaste as Wheatley took out a packet of cheap cigarettes. He lit one, relishing the taste of the smoke as he inhaled. Let the silly young basket babble on, he thought to himself. At least this is better than being stuck in that office.

'I've told you in my last report, he appears to be making progress,' said Wheatley carefully. 'He's found out quite a lot already about what Landis might be up to in there.'

'But no hard evidence as yet?'

'Not as yet sir, but I have confidence that he will find some.'

'Very well, tell him to keep going as planned.'

'Really, sir?' asked Wheatley in surprise. He had assumed that Shaw was about to be pulled off the case and they would have to start again from scratch.

'You said what you were going to say would shock me,' he added. 'That's more of a pleasant surprise. I thought you were about to pull him.'

'I haven't finished yet,' said Fellowes, and then waited for a man with a sandwich board who was handing out tracts to walk past them. On the board was written 'HIS JUDGEMENT COMETH AND THAT RIGHT SOON'.

'I've had a consultation with my inner circle,' he continued.

'The ones I'm not supposed to know about,' said Wheatley.

'Quite. And we have come to the conclusion that once your Mr Shaw has found us the evidence we need, he will be of no further use to this department.'

'I don't quite follow, sir.'

'Have you heard of Thomas à Beckett, Major?'

'Some old priest who upset the king and they bumped him off for it, I think. What's that got to do with…'

'If Landis is to work for the British government at a high level,' interrupted Fellowes, 'we cannot risk him being exposed for anything…untoward…in the courts or, God forbid, the press.'

'But Mr Shaw wouldn't go blabbing to the papers!'

'Perhaps not. But there is also a chance that he could give information about Landis to our enemies. We know they're operating in Cambridge University, for a start. How do we know they don't have influence in the church?'

'That's preposterous!' spluttered Wheatley. 'He

wouldn't sell his country out to some...'

'We cannot risk it,' snapped Fellowes. 'Once Shaw has done his job, he will be of no further use to us *whatsoever*. I shan't put this in writing, for obvious reasons.'

Wheatley shivered slightly as the sun was blotted out by a heavy grey cloud. He suddenly felt in need of a drink and wondered if he could get away from Fellowes for a swift one before the lunch hour ended. The life and light had gone out of the park, and he flicked away his cigarette and shrugged his raincoat back on.

'I think you understand my meaning, Wheatley,' said Fellowes.

'I think I do, sir.'

After Mr Grant had been settled back into his chair, the service took place without further incident, and Ruth did not attempt to make contact with Shaw as before. He noticed, however, that Landis was closely observing her reactions and he got the distinct feeling that both of them were part of some sort of medical observation. It was an unpleasant sensation, and he hurried through the liturgy. The familiar words were spoken almost automatically as he wracked his brains, wondering what to do about the key in his pocket.

Someone had clearly planted it there, but who? It could only have been one of the three people close to him during the incident with Mr Grant. He was an unlikely candidate, so that left Barton, Chivers, or Reeves. One of them, he assumed, must want to help him in some way. But how? What was the key for?

After he had pronounced the final blessing, he felt in his pocket again while removing his cassock. He realised it was not only a key that had been deposited there, but that it had a label attached. He had to examine it, but how? The watchful eyes of the orderlies and of course Landis seemed to be on him the whole time.

'Come along, Mr Shaw,' said Landis jovially. 'Lunch will be starting soon. Time to clear up the magician's table.'

Hiding a look of distaste at the remark, Shaw quickly put away the communion items then turned to Landis.

'May I make use of the facilities before luncheon?' he asked, trying to keep his voice level.

'Certainly,' said Landis. 'You may use my private wash-room. It is just to the right of my office. Strictly speaking I ought to send someone with you, but I think we can waive the rules for you.'

'That is most kind,' said Shaw. 'I shall not be long.'

Once again he felt Landis' eyes boring into him as he walked along the corridor to the reception area. Once secreted inside the lavatory he felt in his pocket and removed the key. His eyes widened when he saw the writing on the little paper label that was attached to it.

'Dr Landis' Office.'

Shaw felt his heart pounding. Either Barton, Chivers or Reeves must be an ally. Was it possible, he wondered, that one of them was some sort of agent or 'undercover' operative? But why give the key to him rather than use it himself? There was no time to mull it over. Landis would soon realise he was missing and send someone to look for him. It was too good an opportunity to waste.

Once he realised the coast was clear, he left the lavatory and crossed the corridor swiftly to Landis' office. With his hand shaking, he unlocked the door and stepped inside. When he had previously been in the room he had noticed a large metal filing cabinet in the corner and he crossed to this immediately. Knowing that such contrivances tended to be noisy, he carefully opened it and looked inside.

It was filled with suspension files and each one had a small tab with a name on it. Hurriedly he thumbed through them, looking for a familiar name…then he found it. Harrington, Eleanor. The file had several hand-written reports and letters in it, all marked confidential. His eyes widened as he quickly scanned through them. Much of it was couched in obscure medical terms but one report caught his eye: 'this patient induced into symptoms of acute paranoia by application of 1.5mg of… – here there was a long chemical name which meant nothing to Shaw – '…secondary treatment with (here followed another obscure drug reference) has proved excellent in keeping patient docile. Will continue to use this method until client no longer requires her to be detained.'

So it was true, realised Shaw. Landis was acting entirely unethically and had kept Eleanor Harrington in Ravenswood against her will – and someone had ordered it.

After a moment's hesitation he snatched the paper from the file and folded it away into his pocket. It might be missed, but a chance like this would never come again. He carefully closed the filing cabinet but then, to his horror, he heard the door of the office open. He looked up to see Reeves staring at him.

He opened his mouth to offer some sort of explanation, but she cut him short.

'There isn't time,' she said quickly. 'Landis has already started to become suspicious and sent me to look for you. You'd better come along with me. I'll tell him you were taken ill.'

'I don't understand,' began Shaw.

'We must hurry,' said Reeves. 'This could be our only chance to get Ruth out before tonight. And this time you've got to make sure she's safe. We can't let what happened to Eleanor happen to her as well.'

'You mean you helped Miss Harrington to...'

'I'll explain later. Come along, do exactly as I say, and try not to look too healthy.'

That was hardly likely, thought Shaw. He felt his face must be as white as a sheet after being discovered. At least, he thought, he had found out who his ally was.

A few moments later they arrived in the dining room and Landis looked up from his meal.

'Mr Shaw,' he said brightly. 'We were beginning to think you might have got lost.'

'He was sick in the lavatory,' said Reeves with a look of disgust on her face. 'I suspect he has mild food poisoning.'

'I am very sorry to hear that,' said Landis. 'Would you like me to examine you, Mr Shaw?'

'No need, thank you, Doctor,' said Reeves briskly. 'What he needs is to lie down. He has a long bicycle ride back to the village and I don't think he's in a fit state at the moment.'

'Of course,' said Landis. 'There is a couch in my office if you would like to rest there, Mr Shaw.'

Shaw was about to answer in the affirmative, hoping it might give him an opportunity to take another look in Landis' filing cabinet, but before he could speak, Reeves stepped in.

'I think not, doctor,' she said. 'We don't want any more accidents, do we? I suggest he lies down in room four at the front. That is currently vacant and has a commode in it.'

'Very well,' said Landis, in a tone which suggested he was already bored of the subject. 'Stay as long as you wish, Mr Shaw,' he continued. 'I do hope it wasn't that bread and wine you consumed that made you ill.'

Shaw was about to say that nobody could become ill from consuming the body and blood of Jesus Christ, but checked himself. Now was not the time for religious pride. He smiled wanly and allowed Reeves to lead him down the corridor to room four.

Once they were safely inside, Reeves pointed to the bed. 'You'd better lie down,' she said. 'There are hidden spyholes in all the doors. That's how I knew Ruth had passed you a message. I couldn't see it though. I take it she asked you to help her escape?'

Shaw nodded, and opened his mouth to speak, but Reeves checked him. 'Please, we must be quick. I can't stay here too long or Landis will get suspicious again. I enabled Eleanor to escape by leaving the door keys and my car key where she could find them. Dropping hints about how the car started, and so on. But that won't work with Ruth. She lacks Eleanor's courage and she'll need to be helped.'

'But Miss Reeves,' began Shaw, 'I must tell you that I am working for – for those concerned with Ruth's safety. I managed to find evidence in Dr Landis' filing cabinet that...'

'These people you are working for,' said Reeves, 'are they able to get Ruth out before 6pm tonight?

'I fear not,' said Shaw. 'They are in London. I would have to present the evidence to them, and then...who knows? We could try the police,' he added weakly. Then he wished he had not said it. For if Chief Inspector Ludd could not be reached on the telephone, or worse, refused to be involved, what then?

'The police won't touch this place,' said Reeves. 'Believe me I've tried before.'

'But why must she leave by 6pm?' said Shaw. 'I am confident my...associates...would be able to get here by tomorrow, in which case...'

'No, that's too late,' said Reeves. 'At 6pm Landis is going to perform a procedure on Ruth which will either kill her or turn her into a vegetable. He's mad, quite mad. There's only one thing for it. We'll have to get her out ourselves.'

'I must know if Barton is an ally also,' said Shaw. 'I am certain he was once a good man.'

'He may have been once,' said Reeves. 'I'm guessing you recognised him from his preaching days.But that's all gone now. Landis saw to that.'

'You mean he...'

'Yes. He worked here as an orderly and had terrible headaches from his time in the ring. He was Landis' first guinea pig. He operated on him and cured the headaches.'

'That explains the scar on the side of his head,' said Shaw.

Reeves nodded. 'But the procedure destroyed any belief in a higher power. Any morality, except obedience to orders from Landis. Landis couldn't help bragging about it to me. We won't get any help from Barton. I'm pretty certain Landis sent him off to kill Eleanor.'

'I fear you are correct,' said Shaw. 'But what do you propose we do?'

'I go home just before six – I'm the only member of staff who doesn't live on the premises, apart from the daily who does the meals and cleaning. At 5.45, I take Ruth her medication in her room. Barton will be on the door, and I'll tell him that I'm going to check on you before I go. But instead of me leaving her room, I give Ruth my hat and coat to wear. The ruse worked with Eleanor and they won't expect it to happen twice. She will wait in here, as it's the room nearest the door. I shall previously have told Landis I am taking you home in my motor car as you are still unwell and that you will arrange to have your bicycle collected later. Is that clear?'

Shaw nodded. 'You mean Miss Leigh-Ellison will drive your motor car? Are you sure she knows how? I alas have never learned.'

'Good point,' said Reeves. 'I have no idea if she can drive. Look here, I know. There is a fire escape at the back of the building. It's kept locked, of course, but I have the key. Once you and Ruth get into my motor car, all one of you need do is start the engine. It's too risky to just sit and wait as that may attract attention. It's the blue Wolseley under the large pine tree. There's a button marked 'start' on the dashboard so you won't miss it. Then I shall come down the fire escape and out from behind the house and will hopefully be able to enter the car undetected, and drive us away. Gauge is usually on the gate and he's the laziest of the lot, and won't bother checking. All clear?'

'Clear,' said Shaw.

'Good,' she said. 'I'd better get back now. You just rest and try to look ill, just in case anybody checks on you using the spyhole. It's two now, make sure you're ready to go by 5.45.'

Shaw nodded. 'But why are you doing this, Miss Reeves? Why are you helping me?'

'Landis is a fiend,' she said. 'He took advantage of me. I don't mean…like that…I mean, he found out I had been dismissed from my last job for…for incompetence. I used to drink, but I don't now. It was never made public, but he threatened to use that against me if I told anyone what…what went on here.'

'And the others?' asked Shaw. 'Barton, Chivers and Gauge?'

'Barton, like I said, is a sort of slave of Landis. Chivers is a jailbird and I think Gauge is too. The difference is they *enjoy* the work and don't need to be forced into it. Chivers pushed poor Mr Grant into you while your back was turned, probably as a distraction so that he could slip Landis' key in your pocket as a test.'

'I see,' said Shaw. He shuddered as he remembered Mitch's description of how Eleanor had been pushed off the railway platform. He realised these men were very, very dangerous. 'Thank you for helping me,' he continued. 'There's one more thing. Would you arrange for my wife to be telephoned? She may worry if I am late back.'

'Very well. I will ask to use Dr Landis' telephone.'

'Thank you. You had better go now. I shall pray for us.'

'You do that,' said Reeves grimly. 'We need all the help we can get.'

Chapter Eight

The next three hours passed in an agony of anticipation for Shaw. He dared not even smoke his pipe, lest someone should spy on him through the door and suspect him of shamming. Instead, he spent the time as best he could in earnest prayer. It was one of those rare instances, he realised, when there literally was nothing else he could do but pray.

At one point he must have fallen asleep; how he managed it under such nervous strain was beyond his comprehension, but he felt invigorated rather than drowsy. It began to feel like the last hour before a big push on the Western Front, the dim half-light coming through the barred window, although of dusk rather than dawn, was the same. At least back then, however, he had been able to spend the time in practical ways by talking to the men before they went over the top. Here, he could do nothing but wait.

He checked his watch; almost a quarter to six. He braced himself as he heard the door to his room open; then breathed a sigh of partial relief when he saw it was Ruth.

'Well done,' he whispered. 'Now we must make it to Miss Reeves' car. Do you have her keys?'

Ruth nodded, her face pale but stamped with resolve, and showed Shaw a large door key and what he assumed was the key to Reeves' Wolseley.

He checked that the corridor was clear and then motioned for Ruth to walk with him.

'It's very good of you to run me home, Miss Reeves,' he said brightly as they passed the reception desk. Barton, he was relieved to see, had his head buried in a tabloid newspaper and barely noticed them. 'I feel much better now,' he continued, carefully watching to see if the orderly had noticed them, but his eyes did not move from his paper.

Ruth's hand trembled as she inserted the key in the large lock on the front door. She turned it but there was resistance; she pulled at the door handle but nothing happened. A look of panic crossed her face and and Shaw wondered if she would lose her nerve.

'Sticking again?' called Barton in his ponderous voice. 'Let me have a look.'

Shaw looked round to see the man stand up from his desk. He frowned, and put his newspaper down. Ruth rattled the key in the lock and then suddenly there was a sharp click and the door swung open.

'No need, thank you, Barton,' called out Shaw in what he hoped was a nonchalant tone. He more or less shoved Ruth through the door and then half-dragged her to the blue car in the corner of the driveway. He remembered Landis' office faced out in this direction; would he be watching?

'Keep your head down,' he whispered to Ruth, and his eyes flicked to the windows of Landis' office, but there appeared to be nobody there. He saw movement on the drive; Gauge had gone to open the gates and was pulling one of them open.

Ruth crossed to the driver's door and began to fumble with the key; Shaw dared not help her; if anyone was watching they would think it odd that Reeves would need help. Finally she got the door open and unlocked the passenger door; then they were inside.

'Can you drive?' whispered Shaw.

'I never learned,' said Ruth. 'I told Reeves but she said it didn't matter.'

'Very well,' said Shaw. 'We must start the engine. Now let me see. The key goes in there, I think; that is correct. Now turn it; and press the starter button here.'

Ruth did as instructed and there came the roar of an engine but then a hiccough and the engine cut. The car lurched forward then stopped. Shaw was not certain what had happened but from what little he knew of motor cars, he thought it might have been left in gear. He looked up to see that Gauge had stopped opening the gates, and was looking enquiringly over at them.

'What do I do now?' said Ruth, panic rising in her voice. 'Do I press the button again? What if it cuts out? They'll know something's wrong.'

Shaw made a snap decision. If they did nothing, Gauge would think they had a mechanical fault and might try to help. If they tried again, it might work and give Reeves enough time to get in the car unseen. He looked in the rearview mirror and saw a flicker of movement at the side of the house. Was that Reeves? If so, she would only be able to make it to the car if she knew that Gauge was not looking.

'Yes, try again,' he said quickly.

With a trembling hand Ruth pressed the starter button and the engine roared again but then an instant later cut out as the car stalled once more.

Shaw heard a shout from the gate and looked up to see Gauge beginning to close the gates. Then the driver's side door of the car was flung open and Ruth collided with Shaw as Reeves pushed her hard across the bench seat. Shaw gave a brief prayer for thanks that the car did not have separate seats, which would have wasted precious seconds. The door slammed shut and the engine howled as Reeves pushed the accelerator pedal to its maximum. A hailstorm of gravel flew up and dashed the wings of the car as it surged forward.

Gauge had by now closed one of the gates, and over the roar of the engine Shaw could hear the insistent clamour of an electric alarm bell.

'We'll never make it!' screamed Ruth, as Gauge began to close the other gate.

'Hold on!' shouted Reeves, and Shaw felt himself knocked back into the seat as the car accelerated to twenty miles per hour. A moment later Shaw felt himself hurled forward onto the dashboard; there was an explosion of shattering glass and tortured metal, and then a shower of water over the bonnet as the radiator cap burst. The car had become wedged in the narrow space between the two gates. The engine cut out and Shaw's vision swam.

The next thing he knew, the car doors were opened and he felt his arms almost wrenched from their sockets as ape-like hands dragged him out.

'I'm so glad to hear your telephone has been re-connected, Mrs Keating,' said Mrs Shaw. 'I wonder, might I have a word with your husband?'

A moment later Mrs Shaw heard the reassuring voice of Dr Keating on the telephone.

'You're in luck, Mrs Shaw,' he said. 'The GPO managed to mend our wires early. I thought it must be the luck of the Irish but it was because they found out I'm a doctor, would you believe it? Now, what can I do for you?

'It sounds silly,' said Mrs Shaw, 'but I'm worried about Lucian.'

'Why so?'

'He was administering Holy Communion at Ravenswood today, and I received a telephone call from a nurse there saying he had been taken ill and that she would run him home in her motor car.'

'Wait just a moment. Why on earth was he giving communion in that place?'

'Oh, didn't he mention he'd been appointed Chaplain?'

'No he did not and I must say it's a surprise. The last I heard of that place was Mr Shaw saying it was being looked into by the relevant authorities.'

'That's all he said to me, too,' said Mrs Shaw, feeling somewhat disloyal to her husband, but her concern for his safety over-rode such fine marital quibbles.

'Hmm, I wonder if the "relevant authorities" just happen to be your husband in some capacity. Is that possible?'

'It could be. He's had some rather strange telephone

calls recently. Of course, one doesn't like to eavesdrop, but...'

'Well, let's not assume anything for now. What sort of illness did the nurse mention?'

'She – the nurse that is – said it was a stomach upset. Probably mild food poisoning. But, well, Lucian is hardly ever ill, and he's certainly never had any problems with his digestion.'

'And he's not back yet?'

'No. The nurse said she would bring him home about six o'clock but it's half past now and there's no sign of him. I tried telephoning, but the operator said there's no number listed for any place called Ravenswood.'

'That's a bit odd,' said Keating. 'And given what we suspect about Ravenswood, you think there might be more to it?'

'I suppose so. You see, I know Lucian's up to something, but he won't tell me what. He never does, until it's all too late. He doesn't like to worry me, I suppose, but that just has the effect of worrying me even more. Oh dear, I'm rather babbling on. Perhaps I shouldn't have called.'

'Not at all, Mrs Shaw, not at all,' said Keating in his best bedside manner. 'You were right to telephone. I'm assuming you called me rather than bother that Chief Inspector...Ludd, was it now? It's not exactly a police matter, is it?'

'You are correct, I did not want to involve the police,' said Mrs Shaw. 'After all it's only a *feeling* that something's wrong, and one can't simply telephone a Chief Inspector about that.'

'There's such a thing as women's intuition Mrs Shaw,

I wouldn't deny that but I don't think we've a need for the police just yet. Now I tell you what we'll do. I've a minor operation to perform on a patient at home in the village shortly. If Mr Shaw still isn't home by, let's say eight o'clock, because I'll be finished by then, call again and I'll run you up there in the car. If there's anything untoward going on – and I don't think in a million years there will be – we'll telephone for the Chief Inspector.'

'That's very kind of you, Dr Keating. I do feel relieved.'

'All part of the service and no charge,' said Keating jovially.

After he had replaced the telephone receiver, he stood for a moment in thought, then went into his consulting room and opened his medical bag. He took down a certain bottle from a shelf, placed it in the bag, then left the house.

Shaw tried to move his arms again but it was useless. Instead of being held in place by simian-like hands, his wrists were now tightly manacled by thick leather straps, his ankles likewise.

After Reeves had crashed the car, all three of them had been manhandled back into the house. Landis had ordered Ruth to be locked in her room but Shaw and Reeves had been half dragged, half shoved into the basement and both of them had been strapped to sinister-looking couches. The door had been slammed shut and they were left alone in the half-light filtering down from a barred window at ceiling level.

Shaw looked around the room. It was large, covering most of the floor area of the house, and had presumably originally been a servants' kitchen of some sort. But now it had all the acoutrements of a laboratory; there were benches covered with vials, retorts and other apparatus. Everything was completely clean and modern, and yet there was something deeply sinister about the place. A large lamp, of the type one sees in operating theatres, hung from the ceiling.

Shaw was able to raise his head and look across to Reeves.

'Are you all right, Miss Reeves?' he asked.

'Perfectly,' she replied crisply. 'I was only slightly grazed in the accident. I'm sorry it was such a failure.'

'You did your best,' said Shaw. 'Now we must concentrate our efforts on escape once more.'

Reeves laughed bitterly. 'There's no escape from here, Mr Shaw. This is the end.'

'We cannot simply do nothing,' said Shaw, his mind working feverishly. 'There must be a way to…'

He stopped talking when he heard a door being unlocked. There was a flight of stairs to his left, which presumably led to the hallway above. Down it came Landis, followed by Barton and Chivers.

'Has Gauge removed the car?' asked Landis.

'He's just shifting it now, chief,' said Chivers. 'I told him he's to come down here when he's hidden it behind the house.'

'Very good,' said Landis. 'Search Mr Shaw's pockets. I want that key back, and anything else he might have of mine.'

Chivers leered as he shoved his hands into Shaw's pockets. 'Here's his wallet, chief,' he said brightly. 'One, no, two quid inside. Might as well take it.'

'Don't be ridiculous,' said Landis. 'Put it back and do as I instructed.'

Chivers shrugged. 'Here's the key,' he said, fishing it out of Shaw's jacket pocket. 'And there's a letter here and all.'

Landis took the key and looked at the letter.

'As I expected, Mr Shaw,' he murmured as he examined the letter, 'you fell rather neatly into my little trap.'

Shaw felt cold horror rising into his throat. He had been a fool – an utter fool. He realised Reeves had been right about the key.

'You mean the key was deliberately placed in my pocket.'

'That is correct. Chivers planted it, as obviously as possible, whilst Reeves was helping him to restrain Grant. The old fool provided a useful distraction.'

'He's always good for a lark, that one,' sniggered Chivers.

'Silence!' barked Landis. 'I had my suspicions about you, Mr Shaw, from the moment you arrived at this establishment.'

'I fail to see in what way I was acting suspiciously,' said Shaw.

'Come, come…' chided Landis. 'It was your noble but misguided attempt to help Miss Harrington that gave you away. Barton was watching the doctor's house and saw her climb out of the window. He followed her into the lane by the side of the house and that was when you appeared. Is that correct, Barton?'

A simpleton's grin appeared on the orderly's face. 'That's right,' he said proudly. 'I saw him through the hedge while I was following that girl to the station, but he never noticed me!'

Shaw cursed himself. It had been Barton's footsteps he had heard behind the hedge outside Keating's house. He had blundered around outside the bathroom window, assuming he was undetected, whilst all the time he had been seen by one of Landis' men! That explained also the strange look of recognition that Barton had given him when he had first appeared at Ravenswood.

As if to confirm this, Landis spoke again. 'Barton recognised you when you first came here and reported to me. Your appearance was just too convenient, it seemed. I therefore gave you some rather stodgy bait in the form of a key and some easily accessible confidential files, and you took it. That also gave me the opportunity to root out another traitor. Reeves.'

'You're mad, Landis,' said Reeves in a tired voice. 'Why don't you just get this over with?'

Landis ignored the remark and continued talking. 'I told Reeves that I was suspicious about how long you were absent from the dining room. I knew you must have found the key and were searching my office, but when she did not report this to me, this confirmed she was assisting you. I was reasonably certain she had enabled Eleanor Harrington to escape, but I could not prove it.'

'And so you ordered Barton to kill her,' said Shaw with disgust. Suddenly that gave him an idea.

'Barton, you were once a man of God,' said Shaw. 'Yes, I heard you preach. You were very good. The Holy Spirit breathed from you with every utterance. God has not left you; He will forgive you if you…

'Save your breath,' said Landis. 'He isn't troubled by any of that nonsense anymore, are you, Barton?'

The orderly shook his head, looking blankly at Shaw almost as if he were not there.

'You will hang for this, Landis,' said Shaw sadly. 'You all will, under the principle of joint enterprise.'

'You are in no position to make threats, Mr Shaw,' said Landis. 'Before we begin, I would be interested to know who you are working for.'

Shaw said nothing.

'No matter,' said Landis airily. 'You will soon tell me all I wish to know anyway.'

'I suppose you intend to torture me,' said Shaw.

'Tch, tch, Mr Shaw, this is not the middle ages! I realise the church, of course, had a fondness for torturing its enemies but such things, like your religion itself, have no place in the modern world. I intend to deal with you quickly and cleanly.'

'You are going to kill me, is that it?' asked Shaw, trying to control the tremor in his voice. 'I am not afraid to die, for I know I will rise again in glory. But you, all of you, if you persist in this, will be cast into the uttermost darkness…'

'Do carry on preaching, Mr Shaw,' said Landis amiably. 'It will be your last chance. In a few hours you will have lost all interest in it.'

'I…I don't understand,' said Shaw.

'He's going to alter part of your brain,' said Reeves

bluntly. 'Just as he did with Barton. That's it, isn't it, Landis?'

'In crude terms, yes,' said Landis as he strolled up and down between the two couches, his hand behind his back as if speaking in a lecture theatre. 'I have developed a technique, Mr Shaw, of curing the human mind of all imbalances and illnesses. Such an achievement has been the holy grail, if you'll pardon the expression, of alienists throughout the ages. I have partly achieved it through chemical means – pills and injections – but those are expensive and only partially effective. My procedure is quick, cheap and has a one hundred percent permanent success rate.'

'Apart from the poor devils who die from it,' said Reeves.

'Shut up!' barked Landis.

'Want me to give her a slap, chief?' asked Chivers.

'That will not be necessary,' said Landis, regaining his temper. 'It is true there have been...failures, but that is because the subjects were elderly and in poor health. Ruth Leigh-Ellison was to be my first success, but I shall save her for later. A genuine clergyman is a far better subject.'

'I don't see why,' said Shaw, 'but if you release Miss Leigh-Ellison and Miss Reeves, I am willing to...undergo this procedure. Is that a bargain?'

'Such noble sentiments!' mocked Landis. 'I suppose you think you are Jesus Christ Himself. Well, you are nothing of the kind, Mr Shaw. You are just a rather simple, grubby little country parson and soon you will not even be that.'

'How can you possibly...' began Shaw, but Landis cut

him off.

'My procedure, Mr Shaw, does not only cure mental illness but it also destroys the delusion of religious belief. It nullifies the section of the human mind which produces such useless fantasies.'

'So you spare the body, but kill the spirit?' said Shaw.

'Exactly,' said Landis, clapping his hands together. 'The coming race – the master race that I will help create – has no need of religion. Only total obedience to the state.'

'You're going to do this to anyone and everyone if you can, aren't you, Landis? Not just the mentally ill.' said Reeves.

'Of course,' said Landis. 'Those suffering mental illness will be the first to benefit, because society already sees them as useless outcasts. But when such people are rehabilitated, society will see the benefits of my work. In the near future it will become as routine a procedure as childhood innoculations, and will produce a fully and efficiently ordered society.'

'And you'll be one of the ones giving the orders, of course,' said Reeves coldly.

Landis clicked his fingers. 'Gag her,' he said in a bored voice. Chivers grinned and violently tore the sleeve of Reeves' blouse off then shoved it into her mouth.

'Miss Reeves can watch the procedure,' said Landis, 'knowing that it will be her turn next.'

'Dr Landis,' said Shaw rapidly, 'you asked me who I was working for. Suffice it to say I have acquaintances in the police.'

'I thought as much,' said Landis, 'Some foolish

detective poking his nose where it should not go; presumably the one who visited here. I have influence over the police, which is why I have been left alone and why he has not returned. Certain...high ranking officials are interested in my work. I have but to snap my fingers and they will do my bidding!'

Shaw felt despair growing within him. By 'high ranking officials' did he mean someone like Major Wheatley? If so, that meant there was no earthly power that could stop his evil work.

'There will be nothing for the police to find out anyway,' continued Landis. 'You will succumb to a fever – the procedure has that effect – and in a few days will be quite well again with no memory of what has happened. A small scar, covered by your hair, will be explained by the fact that you fell while suffering from the fever. But any religious faith you have will have quite disappeared. I expect you will need to look for another job.'

Landis chuckled to himself and pulled across a metal trolley covered in surgical instruments. Upon it was a large metallic pillar, with various cables emanating from it.

'You forget that Miss Reeves telephoned my wife,' said Shaw. 'If she comes here looking for me...'

'Let her come,' said Landis. 'That is part of the plan. The stomach complaint Reeves mentioned will be part of the symptoms of the brain fever you are about to contract. There will be no reason for anyone to become suspicious. Now, enough talking. Let me explain what will happen. You are familiar with trepanning?'

'Drilling a hole in the skull,' said Shaw grimly. A

practice of quacks and charlatans since time immemorial.'

Landis ignored the remark, and swung a metal arm from out of the pillar on the trolley. On the end of it was an electric drill. It had the look of a dentist's drill only with a much larger bit on the end.

'This device is of my own design, and is rather clever, though I say it myself. You will feel only moderate pain as the skull is penetrated, but then nothing. It only takes a few minutes, and then once the fever is over you can take your place in the coming new society.'

'Now settle back, Mr Shaw,' continued Landis as he flicked a switch, and the drill buzzed into life. It sounded like an angry hornet, and Shaw looked over to see a look of dull satisfaction on Barton's face. Chivers' mouth was twisted into a sinister grin and he watched intently, licking his lips.

Shaw swallowed back the impulse to scream, and strained at the leather restraints on his hands and feet. He had told the truth when he had said he did not fear death, but this was some thing far worse – a living death, without God, without faith, without hope.

He silently prayed. *'Into thy hands I commend my spirit...'*

The drill edged closer.

Ruth sat in her room, rubbing the bruises on her arms made by Barton when he almost carried her bodily into her room. He had slammed the door shut and locked it, and then she had heard the sounds of the other residents being herded into their rooms – their cells, if truth be told.

She guessed what was going to happen. Whatever hellish fate Landis had in mind for her was presumably going to be carried out on Reverend Shaw and Reeves instead; she had seen them being dragged down into the basement by Gauge and Chivers as Barton dragged her upstairs.

She took a deep breath; there was still a chance. Reeves had given her the big bunch of keys and she had secreted them in her coat pocket, but Barton, in his rush to lock her in her room, had neglected to search her. She grinned as she rummaged through the large bunch, realising that each key had a small label attached with the room number printed on it. She could just about see into the front drive from her small barred window, and saw Gauge attempting to push Reeves' ruined motor car away from the front gate. It was clearly hard work, as even a giant like him was struggling. Good, she thought. That meant there was only Landis, Barton and that filthy little cad Chivers in the building.

She unlocked her door and checked the corridor; nobody seemed to be about. She had no real plan, only a desperate desire to cause as much disruption as possible. If she could just cause a distraction for a few moments, that might be enough to enable her, Shaw or Reeves to get away.

Stealthily she trotted along the corridor, trying not to make too much noise, and located the orderlies' room at the back of the house. She fished out of her coat pocket the box of matches, thanking her lucky stars that she had had the foresight to swipe them from Shaw's communion table.

The room shared by the three orderlies had the sparseness of a barrack-room, alleviated only by tattered pin-ups on the walls. There was a pile of boxing magazines and a bottle of whisky on a table. She dragged the sheets and blankets off the beds and dumped them on the floor, then scattered the magazines on top. She poured the whole bottle of whisky over the heap, then opened the window as far as it would go.

So far so good, she thought. Hurriedly she left the room then checked the fire escape; she was relieved to find that Reeves had not locked it from the outside when she had previously tried to escape through it. She then opened each of the patient's doors in turn. The faces of the poor lunatics looked up at her in confusion, so she went into Mr Murchison's room, thinking him probably the most lucid of the group.

'Come along, Mr Murchison,' she said briskly. 'We're going for a walk in the garden. You'd like that, wouldn't you?'

'Oh yes,' said Mr Murchison brightly. 'But have they made you a nurse, Miss, ah, I forget your name.'

'Yes that's right,' said Ruth quickly, realising he had noticed she was still wearing Reeves' uniform. 'They've promoted me. Now come along. I'm putting you in charge of the others. Make sure they stay in the garden. But we must be quiet! It's a sort of game, you see.'

'Oh good, I do so love games!' exclaimed the poor man. Ruth smiled as enthusiastically as she could while she assembled Miss Layton, Mrs Dalby and Mr Grant, and bustled them down the fire escape stairs. She then locked the door so that they would not be able to get back in, and hurried back to the orderlies' room.

After two failed attempts to strike a match due to trembling hands, she finally succeeded. The pile of bedding and magazines, aided by the highly combustible whisky, caught light far more quickly than she expected. A sheet of blue flame shot across the floor, setting the rug alight, and smoke began to fill the room. Coughing and spluttering, she hurriedly left the room and locked the door.

Cautiously she peeped out of one of the barred windows to see that Gauge was still slowly pushing the Wolseley to the far end of the drive; one of the wheels appeared to be damaged and he was making slow progress.

Smoke now began to drift along the corridor from under the orderlies' door and Ruth fancied she heard the crackle of flames from within. As quietly as she could she went downstairs, at each turn expecting to be grabbed by one of the orderlies, but none seemed to be about. The front desk was unmanned, and the drawing room and dining room deserted. Cautiously she listened at the door and heard indistinct voices from far below, and the noise of something that sounded unpleasantly similar to a dentist's drill.

The air in the lobby was now misty with smoke, and her eyes began to smart. She desperately tried to think what to do next. Any minute now, she guessed, Gauge would spot the smoke billowing out of the orderlies' window, or one of the patients would wander around to the front. She had only a few moments left. Then she looked to the opposite wall of the hallway, by the door to the lavatory and Landis' office, and saw something that made her grin with excitement. Rapidly she rammed home the large bolts on the front door and then crossed to the wall where, next to a conical fire-syphon, there was a little red glass-fronted box marked 'in case of fire break glass', with a small hammer attached to it on a chain. She then took the little hammer and, with almost childish glee, used it to smash the glass.

Immediately the air was filled with the insistent sound of an electric fire bell, and she heard heavy footsteps on the cellar stairs. After a moment's hesitation she took the fire-syphon from the wall and stood next to the cellar door.

Landis looked up as he heard the din of the electric fire bell over the sound of his drill. It was a hair's breadth away from Shaw's head, and every fibre of his body was strained in anticipation of its contact. But then Landis swung the drill away and switched it off.

'What the devil is that racket?' he exclaimed.

'The electric fire bell, chief,' said Chivers. 'Probably gone wrong again. Want me to switch it off?'

'Of course,' sighed Landis. 'How can I possibly carry out a delicate procedure such as this with that noise going on?'

'Righto,' said Chivers, and trotted up the steps to the basement. Shaw, although he could not see him, could hear him open the door, and the noise of the electric bell grew louder. But there was another sound, a banging and hammering noise and a muffled shouting from somewhere far off. What on earth was happening? Dared he believe rescue was on its way?

Before he could consider the matter further, he heard another sound; a sickening thud of something heavy connecting with human bone. There was a crash, and out of the corner of his eye he saw Chivers' inert body fall to the bottom of the steps as limp and heavy as a sack of coal.

Chapter Nine

Keating frowned as he brought his car to a halt at the front gate of Ravenswood. Darkness had fallen now and the old house had the air of an abandoned mausoleum. He shuddered at the thought of anyone being locked up in such a place.

He opened the car door and immediately caught a whiff of smoke, as if there were a bonfire nearby, but why should anyone light a bonfire in such a place as this? He also noticed a car, its front smashed in, parked halfway along the drive at an angle. Somewhere in the distance, an electric bell seemed to be ringing.

'There's something I don't like about this,' he said. 'Mrs Shaw, will you stay in the car a moment? I'll come and fetch you when I've got hold of your husband.'

'You don't think there's any danger?' asked Mrs Shaw nervously.

'I don't think so,' said Keating, 'But from what we know of this place it's best to be careful. Keep the door locked when I close it. That's right, that little catch there. I'll only be two ticks.'

He picked up his medical bag from the back seat and walked through the open gates. Up ahead, the sky seemed brighter than it should be, and there was a yellow-orange glow emanating from the rear of the building. Then he gasped as a figure loomed out of the darkness of some trees by the side of the drive.

'Are you the reinforcements?' asked a refined voice. 'Grant, at your service, sir. Wellington has asked for more men, as the cavalry are outflanked. Waterloo must be won at all costs.'

Keating immediately realised the man was insane, and looked around to see other figures wandering in the shadows.

'Yes, yes, I'm the reinforcements, Mr Grant,' said Keating hurriedly, trying to sound as reassuring as he could. 'Now, you wait here and don't leave the, ah, the battlefield. There's a good fellow.'

The man nodded enthusiastically and gave a salute as Keating turned about and ran back to the car.

He tapped quickly on the door and Mrs Shaw opened it.

'Mrs Shaw, do you know how to drive a motor car?' he asked.

'Why, I did have lessons some years ago, but...'

'Very good. It'll come back to you. Here, now, let me start her up. That's it. Quickly now, into the driving seat. That's right, feet on the pedals. Clutch down and into gear. You're there. Now, drive as quickly as you can back to the surgery and telephone for the fire brigade. I think the house is on fire.'

An expression of alarm crossed Mrs Shaw's face. 'But what about Lucian, oh, I can't leave him...!'

'Mrs Shaw, listen to me,' said Keating with calm urgency. 'I'm sure he'll be all right, but someone has to go for help. And while you're there telephone for the police as well, just in case.'

'But why should the police...'

'Mrs Shaw, go please, now.'

Mrs Shaw merely nodded and the car surged away, lurched momentarily with a clash of gears, but then it pulled away smoothly onto the road and was swallowed up by the dark.

Keating strode quickly on to the drive and pushed the gate closed behind him, hoping it might keep the poor lunatics inside. Then he saw a figure hammering at the front door. He heard a deep, coarsely-accented voice bellowing.

'Open this ruddy door! Can't you see the place is on fire, and someone's let out the blasted...I said get away from me, you old witch!'

The man pushed away an elderly woman who was tugging at his sleeve. Another patient, guessed Keating. The woman hurried away and stood at some distance, watching the orange glow at the rooftop with a worried expression.

Then the man turned towards Keating and instantly he recognised who it was. The bigger of the two orderlies who had come to his surgery in pursuit of Eleanor Harrington. And now, Eleanor Harrington was dead.

He felt cold fear rise in his chest as he realised the man had seen him. 'Hi!' yelled the man hoarsely. 'What d'you think you're doing here? This is private, clear off out of it!'

Something was clearly very wrong and Keating instinctively realised he would not be able to bluff his way past the man. Instead, he ducked behind a pine tree and hurriedly fumbled in his bag. Anger gave him courage; this man had tried to invade his home and he was not going to show any mercy to him. He opened the bottle he had taken from his surgery earlier, and with shaking hands, poured a quantity of liquid onto some cotton wool.

Seconds later the man stopped on the other side of the tree and swore loudly. 'I'll soon sort you out. You're that blasted bog-trotting doctor ain't you? The one that stopped us getting our 'ands on that stuck up little…'

He did not manage to finish the sentence. Keating blind-sided him, feinting a jump to his left, but then he swooped to the right. With his left hand he grabbed the man's left ear, although he could barely reach it; and used it as a hand-hold to jerk his cannon ball of a head backwards so far his neck cracked. He then with his right hand forced the cotton-wool pad across the man's nose and mouth and pushed as hard as he could.

He felt himself bodily lifted off the ground as the giant's hands clamped on his arm and heaved. The man gave a muffled roar but Keating held on with the persistence of a terrier fighting with a giant rat. The man's bellows became weaker and high-pitched, like a boy's voice, and then his eyes rolled upwards into his head. He then gave out a sort of half yawn, half yelp, and crashed forward onto the drive, unconscious.

'Good old chloroform,' muttered Keating as he satisfied himself the man was out cold. 'I'll probably get struck off for doing that, but by God it'll be worth it.'

'He's dead...' exclaimed Barton, as he looked down at Chivers' inert body at the foot of the basement stairs. Shaw struggled to keep his head at a sufficiently high angle to see what was going on, as Landis strode rapidly to the stairs, his white coat flapping behind him.

'Nonsense, he's breathing,' he snapped. 'He must have slipped and hit his head, the damned fool. Put him over there by the wall until he comes round. That's it.'

Shaw fancied he could smell smoke, but nobody in the room had lit a cigarette. There was also a muffled banging sound coming from somewhere upstairs, as if someone were pounding on the door. Was there a chance that they might be rescued? He dared not raise his hopes, but he began to feel new strength surging through him, and as discreetly as he could, he began to strain against the leather wrist restraints. If he could just get one hand free!

'I can smell smoke,' said Barton slowly, as if struggling to find the right words. 'And someone's banging on the door.'

'Probably that idiotic woman in the kitchen has left something on the stove,' said Landis impatiently. 'Go and see to it.'

Barton lumbered slowly up the stairs, and Shaw heard the basement door open and close. The muffled banging continued, but Landis merely looked over Shaw and smiled.

'You look tense, Mr Shaw,' he said. 'Never mind. It will soon all be over, and you will have nothing further to worry about, ever again.'

He adjusted the drill and flicked the switch.

This time Ruth waited until Barton had closed the basement door, and then, from her hiding place behind the door, she brought the heavy fire syphon down on his head. She was only able to manage it on tiptoes and stretching her arms until they felt as if they should pop out of their sockets.

He slumped to his knees. She could scarcely believe it had worked a second time. She had already managed to knock out Chivers; he had fallen backwards back into the basement and she had quickly slammed the door shut behind him. The people in the basement must, she decided, have thought it an accident otherwise Barton would not simply have walked out of the door without a care in the world.

She watched with satisfaction as he clutched his head and groaned. But he was not completely unconscious. Should she hit him again? What if she killed him? Despite her anger and hatred of those who had imprisoned her, she did not think she was capable of cold blooded murder. Instead, she left Barton writhing on the floor and ran to the front door.

Someone was pounding on it and shouting indistinctly, and she unbolted it and flung it wide open. It was a man she did not recognise; but she somehow instinctively felt she could trust him.

The smoke was now billowing down from the staircase and flames were beginning to creep across the ceiling of the hallway. The man looked up in alarm and then at Ruth.

'Ah, you're a nurse,' he exclaimed. 'I'm a doctor, Dr Keating. Is anybody else left inside?'

Ruth looked at him blankly. Why did he think she was a nurse? Then she realised; she was still wearing Reeves' coat and hat.

'Answer me, please!' urged Dr Keating. 'If anyone's left inside we have to get them out. I've sent for the fire brigade but they may be some time.'

'Downstairs, in the basement,' said Ruth quickly. 'Landis has got Mr Shaw down there. And Reeves. We tried to escape, but...'

'What do you mean, he's got Mr Shaw...all right, all right,' said Keating, attempting to remain calm as he began to realise that something was very badly wrong. 'And the patients? There are four of them wandering the grounds. Are there any more?'

Ruth wondered whether to admit she, too, was a patient, but thought better of it and shook her head.

'What about the men, the orderlies,' continued Keating. 'Are they still here?'

Ruth looked round to where she had left Barton and then stared in horror as she saw he was not unconscious but had raised himself to his feet and was staggering towards them. Blood poured from his bald head like red yolk oozing from an enormous cracked egg.

'For the Lord's sake, not another one,' breathed Keating, and he fumbled in his medical bag. Barton roared wordlessly and bore down on Ruth. She ran behind Keating and tried to open the door, then recoiled as a sheet of flame shot across it. One side of the hall was now completely alight.

Keating stepped forward holding a bottle and a wad

of cotton wool, but Barton's enormous hand grabbed the container and dashed it to the burning wall, where it exploded in a sheet of flame.

Ruth looked to the staircase; could they get up it? No, the flames were licking around them and the air was black with thick, choking smoke. It would be madness. There was no escape.

Then there was a groaning, cracking sound and an enormous crash as the hall ceiling collapsed.

Shaw strained desperately at the manacle covering his right wrist, reasoning that he would have more strength in that part of his body than elsewhere. He felt a stab of hope as the leather loosened imperceptibly. He must keep trying! Meanwhile, the room had become uncomfortably hot, and he felt perspiration streaming from his body. Coughing as he breathed the smoky air, he called out to Landis, who was adjusting the level of the drill to bring it nearer to Shaw's head.

Shaw shouted to make himself heard over the whining of the trepanning drill and the distant ringing of the firebell.

'You can't seriously expect to operate on me now, Landis! Can't you see the smoke in here? That's more than just a pot burning on the stove!'

'Be quiet!' yelled Landis. 'I must have quiet to work!'

'If you don't care about us, at least care about yourself', said Shaw. 'The house is on fire. Think of your own safety – if you die who will carry on your work?'

A last, desperate appeal to Landis' vanity – would it work? Shaw watched the man's face intently while he struggled imperceptibly with the leather manacle. It was definitely loosening, and now the sweat pouring down his arm acted as a lubricant. He had now worked his hand out almost to the thumb joint. He must make sure Landis did not see it!

A look of doubt crossed Landis' face. 'If I leave you now,' he said, 'I may never have such a suitable subject again. No, it must be done now! A clergyman – a man of God! And I can make you *godless!*'

The gleam of insanity momentarily flashed in his eyes as Shaw, with one last burst of strength, freed his hand from the leather manacle. In a limp, awkward movement he shoved the drill pillar away, but it spun round and caught Landis hard on his shoulder.

He screamed in a peculiarly feminine way as blood and shredded cloth spun outwards. Clutching at the wound he staggered back and then with a roar of rage, grabbed a scalpel and raised it above Shaw's heart.

Then he fell backwards out of Shaw's vision and he strained his neck to see what had happened; the next thing he saw was a man, his face blackened like a minstrel singer, grinning at him, holding a fire syphon in his hand. It was Keating!

'This thing's more effective than ether,' he said, looking admiringly at the extinguisher. 'He'll have a bit of a headache but he'll live. Nurse, would you release this other woman please – quickly now.'

'Keating, thank God!' exclaimed Shaw, rubbing his wrists as the doctor released him. 'But...Nurse...? he asked Shaw in confusion as he looked across the room.

Then he remembered. 'Miss Leigh-Ellison! You're safe!'

'For the moment,' said Ruth grimly. 'And I'm not a nurse,' she said to Keating, as she threw off Grigg's hat and coat on to the floor.

'Come on, Miss Reeves, that's it,' she said, helping the nurse off the couch. 'We've got to get out of here.'

'Haven't we just,' said Keating. 'That great ape in the hallway came for us but a roof beam fell on him – he's done for. We can't get out the front door. Is there any way out down here?' He looked around frantically. 'Can't see one. Right, we'll have to try to make it through the back way. Come on.'

Shaw staggered to his feet and followed Keating, Reeves and Ruth to the foot of the cellar steps.

'What about Landis, and this one?' said Keating, pointing at the prone forms of the doctor and Chivers.

'Leave them,' said Ruth. 'They'd have done the same to us.'

'We must at least try,' said Shaw urgently. 'They must stand trial for their crimes.'

'He's right,' said Keating. 'Death's too easy for this lot. Come on Mr Shaw. You take the little one and I'll take Landis.'

Shaw knelt to try to rouse Chivers, and jumped back as the man leapt to his feet. Shaw realised he must have been shamming, and waiting for his moment to strike. He looked warily at the assembled company, and waved a folding pocket-knife at them.

'All right,' he snarled. 'I don't know how you worked it but you ain't getting me. I'm out of here, see, so you get out of my way.'

'Now look here,' began Keating. Reeves cut him off.

'Let him go,' she said. 'Like a rat leaving a sinking ship.'

Chivers pushed past Reeves and pounded up the stairs.

'Ladies, get out,' cried Keating, bodily pushing Ruth and Reeves up the steps. 'We'll both take Landis, Mr Shaw.'

Shaw nodded but he felt his strength begin to ebb. It was getting hard to breath now and the heat was intolerable, like the hottest Turkish bath one could ever imagine. Both men coughed violently as they went back down the steps to fetch Landis. Then Keating shouted in alarm.

'For heaven's sake, where did he get to?' he shouted. 'He was lying just here.'

'He...must have got out somehow...while we weren't looking...' coughed Shaw. 'Come along, we must make sure the ladies are safe.'

Once upstairs, the smoke was so dense it was like trying to force one's way through heaps of choking, stinging cotton wool. The only illumination was the eerie, flickering beams cast by the wall of fire which barred the front door; Shaw saw two figures up ahead in the corridor past the drawing room.

'There may be a way out here,' he shouted to Keating. 'The doors and windows are barred but there must be a door in the kitchen for the daily!'

The electric fire bell had now stopped; presumably its mechanism had been destroyed by the encroaching flames. But now there was another noise; an ominous groaning, cracking sound. Shaw looked up and saw a spreading black stain on the white ceiling of the corridor, as if a sheet of paper were being held over a candle.

'The laths are about to burn through,' shouted Keating. 'Come on, let's get out!'

They stumbled along the corridor and eventually found a door marked 'kitchen'. A bunch of keys were left in the lock, and the door opened easily. Inside the kitchen the air was clearer, and they found Reeves leaning over the sink breathing heavily. The back door was open, and Shaw took great lungfuls of cool, clean air before speaking.

'Come along, Miss Reeves,' he urged. 'Follow Miss Leigh-Ellison outside, please.'

Reeves stared. 'I thought she was back there with you.'

'But we assumed she was with *you*!' exclaimed Shaw.

'It's as black as night in there,' said Keating. 'She must have collapsed and we walked straight past her. Come on, Shaw.'

Shaw nodded and the two men ran to the kitchen door but Reeves got there first. 'I'll go,' she said. 'You two get out.' Keating and Shaw began to argue but Reeves rushed past them. 'There's no sense us all risking it, for God's sake get out!'

Reeves disappeared into the smoke filled corridor. 'We can't leave her...' shouted Shaw, and moved to open the door, then jumped back as the entire ceiling collapsed in an explosion of fire and black smoke.

Shaw momentarily wondered where he was, and why so many people were talking in his bedroom. Then he felt the touch of light rain on his face and opened his eyes. He was lying on a blanket by the side of the driveway at Ravenswood.

Around him rushed firemen, policemen and men whom he recognised from the village, presumably come out to assist in the rescue. A clanging bell announced the arrival of a fire engine, which parked itself next to three others on the drive, and the men holding on to the sides of the vehicle jumped down and began unravelling hoses.

Shaw felt a spasm of coughing grip him but after a few seconds he could breath relatively normally. He felt an arm around his shoulder and a metal flask was thrust into his hand.

'It's Irish whiskey, so it's twice as good as the Scottish stuff,' said a familiar voice. 'Go on, take a swig. Doctor's orders.'

Shaw gulped from the flask and felt the reviving warmth of its contents flood his stomach. He looked in shock at Keating's face. It was jet black from smoke and dust, with two white patches around the eyes and a pink circle at his mouth. His hair was partly singed and stood up in huge tufts from his head.

'Keating, my goodness,' he exclaimed. 'You look like...like that American singer from the talking pictures.'

'Al Jolson?' roared Keating. 'Sure, you don't look much different yourself! But for the Lord's sake this is no time to start singing!'

'I say, Dr Keating,' said another familiar voice. 'Has

he come round?'

'He's perfectly well, Mrs Shaw,' said Keating. 'Nothing a drop of Jameson's won't cure.

'Oh Lucian, I was so worried about you,' said Mrs Shaw, looking at her husband with concern.

'No need,' said Shaw, as he struggled to his feet and looked about him. There were little groups of fireman training jets of water on the house, and most of the fire now seemed to have gone out.

'Keating,' he asked urgently, 'where are Miss Reeves and Miss Leigh-Ellison?'

'You mean those two from the house?' asked Keating. Shaw nodded.

'Ah, some bad news, I'm sorry to say. After the ceiling collapsed I had to drag you outside as you caught the worst of the smoke. There was no way I could get back inside. But two of the firemen managed it with their axes, and they found the two ladies on the floor. The nurse, Reeves, is it, had dragged the other one to the kitchen door and the firemen got them out. But they found Reeves was dead.'

'The poor woman,' said Shaw, shaking his head. 'Her final act was to help another. And Miss Leigh-Ellison?'

'She's alive – just,' said Keating. 'They've taken her by ambulance to Midchester Hospital. I'll have a look in on her later.'

'What of the poor patients?' said Shaw. 'How many perished in the fire?'

'Ah, there you might be able to help,' said Keating. 'How many residents were there?'

'Five, including Miss Leigh-Ellison.'

'Wait,' said Keating, 'you mean that young, pretty

looking thing was one of the ones locked up in there?'

'Correct,' said Shaw.

'Well, that's a surprise, but anyway, that means all of them got out. We found four of the poor creatures wandering in the grounds. They're being taken to the county asylum until we can work out what to do with them.'

Shaw breathed a sigh of relief. Then he felt a stab of fear as he realised there were others that were unaccounted for. He was about to raise this point with Keating, but before he could, he heard another familiar voice nearby.

'I'm assuming you're well enough to talk, Mr Shaw, as you seem to be doing a fair deal of it already, so I'll have to ask you some official questions.'

'Chief Inspector Ludd,' said Shaw. 'What on earth are you doing here? I thought…'

'You thought I was barred from coming here by the Chief Constable, eh?' said Ludd, as he nodded to Keating and raised his hat to Mrs Shaw. 'Well that was when we had no evidence of any crime being committed. There's nothing to say I can't come and make sure public order's being kept when a major fire takes place in my district.'

'I don't think he's up to answering questions,' said Keating doubtfully.

'Really, Dr Keating, I am perfectly well,' said Shaw. 'What did you wish to ask me, Chief Inspector?'

'One of my men found a big chap, dressed like an orderly, passed out in the driveway. He's come round but says he doesn't remember anything.'

'He won't, for a good while,' exclaimed Keating, and

then clapped his hand to his mouth.

'What's that supposed to mean?' said Ludd.

'Nothing,' said the doctor guiltily.

Ludd gave the man a suspicious glance and turned back to Shaw.

'I've spoken to the chief fire officer from Great Netley and he says they've found two bodies in there. One was a great big fellow who was under a lot of rubble in the hallway.'

'That's the orderly that came for us,' said Keating.'

'Barton,' interjected Shaw. 'A form of justice, perhaps...but did he even know what he was doing when he committed murder?'

'And what's *that* supposed to mean?' asked Ludd.

'Nothing,' said Shaw quickly. 'Who was the other victim?'

'We don't know his name,' said Ludd, 'but he was a little chap with a thin moustache. Ambulance man said he died from smoke inhalation trying to get out through the office.'

'Chivers,' said Shaw. 'And Landis...?'

'The doctor who runs the place?' asked Ludd. 'He's been very helpful in explaining how the whole thing started. Thinks it was a pot on the stove.'

'You mean he's alive...?' asked Shaw.

'Don't look so unhappy about it,' said Ludd. 'I've just been speaking to him.'

Shaw looked across the driveway to where a figure in a white coat, somewhat stained, was talking to a fireman. He turned towards Shaw, and his face held an unmistakeable look of triumph.

Chapter Ten

Why the devil, thought Wheatley, did that fool Fellowes have to choose such daft places in which to meet? The man had presumably been reading too many Bulldog Drummond novels when he should have been working.

This time he had been summoned by 'F' to a little church in a back-street near Victoria station; one of those dark, quiet places that never seem to have anyone in them. He opened the creaking door and peered through the gloom to see a figure seated near the front.

He remembered to take off his hat but couldn't remember what else you were supposed to do; was there some water pot thing you were supposed to stick your fingers in, or was that for the Romans? He shrugged; it was years since he had been in a church and there was nobody around to see, so he decided it didn't matter.

He sat down next to Fellowes, who looked at him askance.

'It's customary to acknowledge the altar,' he said disapprovingly.

'Hello, altar,' said Wheatley with a cheery wave in the direction of the east window, where a portrait of Christ on the cross, heavily embossed with age, hung above a tapestry-clad communion table.

'I meant with a bow,' said Fellowes through gritted

teeth. 'What do you have for me?'

'I didn't bring you any flowers, if that's what you mean, sir.'

'Your manner is beginning to bore me, Wheatley. You know quite well what I mean. The Ravenswood case.'

'You've had my report, sir.'

'I know. But there are certain things one oughtn't to put in reports. That's why I asked you here.'

'Nobody listening, eh?' said Wheatley with a smile. 'Except Him, of course,' he added, pointing to the portrait above the altar.

'A little respect for your surroundings would not go amiss,' said Fellowes with a bored sigh.

'Beg pardon, I'm sure,' said Wheatley, and was amused to see Fellowes visibly wince upon hearing the expression.

'And on the subject of churches,' said Fellowes, looking around to ensure they were still alone, 'how is our dear Mr Shaw?'

'I motored down to Suffolk to see him yesterday, sir. He's recovering at home, but he's not badly hurt.'

'Good, good,' said Fellowes smoothly.

'The only snag is he didn't manage to get any firm evidence against Landis,' continued Wheatley. 'He said there was a filing cabinet full of it, but I had a poke around the wreckage later, and it was all burnt up. Not a scrap of any documents left.'

'Oh dear,' said Fellowes. 'He was rather a waste of time, then, wasn't he?'

'I beg to differ...sir. Landis told him all about his...methods...and was even going to try it out on him if the fire hadn't stopped him. But I reckon Shaw could still give evidence against Landis. After all, he tried to force an operation on him. That might be all that you need to get him to work for you.'

And he'll be more use to you alive than dead in that case, thought Wheatley, holding his breath as Fellowes considered what he had said.

'It would be his word against Landis'', he finally answered. 'Not much of a threat.'

'There's the girl, though,' said Wheatley. 'Miss Leigh-Ellison. She's in a bad way but if she pulls through, she'll corroborate Shaw's story. And there's the other patients, and the orderly that survived, Gauge, he...'

'No, I don't think so,' said Fellowes dismissively. 'Nobody committed to a mental institution would be able to give evidence against their doctor. It would never get near a jury. And that orderly, Gauge, has been promised an extremely generous monthly remittance, on the understanding that he never mentions the name of Landis again.'

'Promised by who, sir?'

'By this department.'

'I don't follow, sir,' said Wheatley, but he was beginning to realise the little sneak had been running rings around him again.

'I met with Dr Landis yesterday at his club,' said Fellowes. 'He's up in London now.'

'Oh yes...?'

'Yes, and it seems his initial reluctance to work for His Majesty's government has eased somewhat. I think your little espionage effort with Mr Shaw rattled him a little. Showed him he's not quite as unassailable as he thinks.'

'I'm glad to hear it,' said Wheatley with relief in his voice. 'So we'll need to keep Mr Shaw on our side, in case we ever need to rattle Landis again, eh?'

'Not *quite*,' said Fellowes quietly. 'We do indeed require the services of Mr Shaw again, but not for much longer.'

Wheatley wondered just what nasty little idea Fellowes had up his sleeve. He did not have to wait long.

'You seem confused, Major, so I shall elucidate. Landis has agreed to give his full co-operation to the government in the field of psychiatric research, on one condition.'

'Which is?'

'He requires a fit and sane test patient. And he believes Mr Shaw has certain…qualities…that make him an ideal candidate. He explained his procedure briefly to me and I think the idea is excellent. He also assures me it will make it highly unlikely that Mr Shaw will ever want to make any accusations against him either.'

'This…procedure…' said Wheatley slowly. 'I thought it was for shell shock. But Mr Shaw said it was…'

'Dr Landis assures me,' said Fellowes, 'it is a brief, simple and painless operation which renders the patient disinclined to thoughts of rebellion; hard working, quick to obey authority, practical-minded and down to earth. In short, it creates model citizens. What, may I ask, is wrong with that?'

Wheatley swallowed. 'Mr Shaw said the procedure would rob people of any religious belief they had. He said it would…'

'Yes?' asked Fellowes impatiently, looking at his watch.

Wheatley struggled for the right words. 'He said it would kill their spirits. Their souls, if you like.'

'Major, are you a religious man?' enquired Fellowes.

'No, but...'

'Exactly. So why on earth would it matter if someone "killed your spirit" if there is no such thing to begin with?'

'It...it just doesn't seem right, sir...'

'Wheatley, it is 1935, not the middle ages. This is an age of *realpolitik*, not religious fantasies. Either the Germans or the Soviets, in a few years – no more than five, I assure you – will have the means to conquer Britain and her Empire. To make slaves of us. Don't you see – Landis' procedure could prevent that? We can build an unstoppable army, munition workers who will never shirk, civilians who will laugh in the face of air raids, children who will joyfully give up their play-time in the service of the state...'

Fellowes had a distant look in his eyes, as if his gaze extended far beyond the portrait of the suffering Christ above the altar. It was the look, thought Wheatley, on the faces of the political zealots one saw on soap boxes at Hyde Park Corner.

'How can we be sure this procedure works?' asked Wheatley.

'Are you a scientist?' asked Fellowes bluntly.

'No sir, but...'

'Then kindly do not presume to question the knowledge of experts.'

'Yes sir. But you realise Mr Shaw won't come quietly,'

said Wheatley, the full horror of what he was being told to do beginning to sink in. 'He'll have to be brought in on some pretext, so that nobody suspects anything.'

'I'm sure it's within your capabilities to think of some excuse to get him to London,' said Fellowes, as he passed a calling card to Wheatley. 'We're setting up a laboratory, but for the present, bring him to this address on Friday at 4pm. It's Landis' London flat. '

'Alone?'

'Yes, the fewer who know about this, the better. Once Shaw is at the flat, Landis will sedate him and then he'll be taken to the laboratory by private ambulance. The operation results in a sort of brain fever, according to Landis, so that's all his family need to be told. And for God's sake don't tell Shaw who he's meeting or he might cut and run.'

Wheatley took the card and examined it.

'All nicely planned out without me, eh? What if I refuse, sir?'

'Why should you?' asked Fellowes with raised eyebrows.

'Perhaps I don't particularly like things like this being arranged behind my back…'

'If I had my way, Wheatley, chaps like you would rise no higher than sergeant-major in some fish-and-chip infantry regiment. Personally I think you are lucky you have any involvement in this case at all, but the Home Secretary has been impressed by some of your recent work and asked me to keep you on, so I must defer to his greater wisdom.'

'That's very nice to hear, sir.'

'As for whether you do what you're told or not, I'm

sure I don't need to remind you what the outcome of a court martial would be,' snapped Fellowes. 'You're still subject to military discipline.'

'Of course sir,' said Wheatley briskly, thinking of a firing squad he had witnessed early one morning in France so many years ago.

'I must be getting sentimental in my old age, sir. Friday afternoon, then.'

'Very good,' said Fellowes, and stood up. He stopped momentarily in the aisle and bowed gracefully towards the altar, then strode out of the church.

'This is becoming something of a habit, Mr Shaw,' said Lady Stoneleigh as she sat down in the sitting room at the vicarage. It was three days after the fire, and he had been pleased to see the expensive calling card brought in to his study on a silver tray by Hettie.

'You are "visiting a cousin" once again?' he asked.

'There is no need for subterfuge this time,' said Lady Stoneleigh, 'hence the reason for me calling here. I have managed to bring my husband round to my way of thinking.'

'Which is?'

'Which is that we should no longer live in fear of what these people might do to us.'

'What made you change your mind?'

'I read the accounts of the fire at Ravenswood in the *Times*, Mr Shaw. Something did not ring true about it. I take it it was not entirely…accidental?'

'I suspect not,' said Shaw.

'And the two employees who died in the fire, were they the ones who threatened us in London?'

'I believe so.'

'And my daughter's killer – was he one of them?'

'The man who I believe carried it out, Barton, is dead.

'That is at least some consolation.'

Shaw shook his head. 'He was merely a functionary. I am not sure he was even fully aware of what he was doing. The man who I believe ordered it – Landis, is still very much alive.'

'Mr Shaw, what exactly was this Dr Landis doing in Ravenswood? Something more than just keeping potentially awkward people out of the way, I assume?'

'Lady Stoneleigh, you will forgive me if I do not divulge any more information. You see, certain parties...legal entities, one might say, have forbidden me from doing so.'

'*Sub judice*, or something of that sort?' she asked with a raised eyebrow.

'Something of that sort, yes.'

'Now it is my turn to ask a question,' said Shaw. 'Can you tell me the name of Ruth's seducer?'

Lady Stoneleigh, with a brittle smile, uttered the name of a prominent member of the Cabinet. 'The man died a few days ago, of natural causes I might add, as you probably read in the newspapers.'

'Ah yes,' said Shaw. 'I think I know who you mean. He was the leader of some sort of "moral crusade", as I recall.'

'You can see why he wanted the whole business kept secret,' replied Lady Stoneleigh. 'I doubt it would serve any purpose to dig it up now. It would only bring pain to his surviving relatives. He cannot be held to account. At least not on this earth.'

'Perhaps you are right,' said Shaw.

'It was partly his death that spurred me on to my decision,' said Lady Stoneleigh. 'Somebody must be held responsible, and that should be Dr Landis. His position will be weakened following the destruction of his hospital and the death of two of his...minions. We are reasonably wealthy, Mr Shaw, and can afford good lawyers. Ones who will not be easily threatened. We intend to begin a civil action against Dr Landis, and this time we shall be prepared. Letters will be deposited with our solicitors to be opened in the event of our deaths, and so on. May we count on your support?'

Shaw thought for a moment, and chewed distractedly on the stem of his pipe. Landis was clearly mad, but he was protected. Chief Inspector Ludd had made it clear that the police had been warned off. He, Shaw, had failed to find the necessary evidence to allow Wheatley's department to stop him. But he must be stopped in some way, that much was clear.

He turned to Lady Stoneleigh and smiled. 'I shall support you to the fullest extent that I am able.'

'Thank you,' said Lady Stoneleigh, standing up. 'And now I shall visit poor Ruth in hospital. I telephoned earlier and was told she is conscious but very tired.'

'I am sure she will appreciate your visit.'

'I intend to reconcile her with her parents when she is well enough,' said Lady Stoneleigh. 'I know what it is like to lose a daughter and there is no reason why Mr and Mrs Leigh-Ellison should suffer in the same way.

May I count on your support in that endeavour also?'

'You may,' said Shaw.

Early on Friday morning, Wheatley dressed in the front bedroom of his semi-detached villa in Turnham Green. He moved quietly, so as not to wake his wife, still asleep in the other bed. He looked down at her and smiled; she was a good woman and despite his pose as a ladies' man he was deeply fond of her.

He had married late in life, and they had no children. But, he reflected, it was his wife that kept him going through all the sordid work he had to undertake. She had only a vague idea of what he did for a living, which was probably for the best, he thought.

After a hurried breakfast he backed his car out of the garage then, at a discreet distance from the house, stopped and checked the slim automatic pistol in his pocket for the second time that morning.

It was early enough to avoid most of the morning traffic blocks in London, and he was soon on the Eastern Avenue and then roaring along the great arterial road which led to Suffolk.

It was a route he was now familiar with – too familiar for his liking. He could not help wondering if the Ravenswood business was all somehow his fault and he began to wish he had never heard the name of Reverend Lucian Shaw.

By mid morning he arrived at Lower Addenham and parked his car in the small carriage-turn outside the vicarage. As he walked to the front door, he fingered the pistol in his pocket, then his hipflask. He considered a quick nip, but decided against it. He needed a clear head for what he was going to have to do. He took a deep breath and rang the bell.

'Good morning, Major Wheatley,' said Shaw brightly as Hettie showed him into the study. 'I received your telegram last night saying you were coming. Fortunately I have just finished Morning Prayer. Would you care for some tea?'

'Ah, no thank you, Mr Shaw,' said Wheatley, turning his hat in his hands as he looked around the room. 'If it's all the same to you, I think we'd best be on our way.'

'Very well,' said Shaw. 'Your telegram only mentioned we would have to undertake a trip. Where to, may I ask?'

'London.'

'I see. I do have a meeting with the parochial church council this evening, so I will need to…'

'Mr Shaw, I can't promise to get you back for that,' said Wheatley. 'You'll appreciate this trip is of the utmost importance, or I wouldn't have asked you.'

'Yes of course. I assume it concerns the Landis case?'

'I'd rather not talk about it here. We can discuss it in the car.'

'Certainly. Very well, let us leave immediately.'

Shaw ushered Wheatley into the corridor and put on his hat and coat, and looked down to see Fraser wagging his tail.

'No, Fraser, you cannot come to London,' he said. ' Go to your mistress.'

Shaw chuckled as the little dog gave him a soulful look and trotted off in the direction of the kitchen.

'Major Wheatley,' he said, looking with concern at the man's face, 'are you quite well? You look rather tired. Are you sure a cup of tea would not...'

'I'm quite all right,' Wheatley said quickly, almost snapping at him. 'It's just I...well I had a bit of a sleepless night last night. I'll be all right once I'm back on the road.'

'Lead on,' said Shaw with a smile, and opened the front door for him.

Wheatley's powerful car made short work of the trip back to London, barrelling along the straight arterial roads and only slowing down to pass through small towns and villages. Wheatley said nothing, but kept his eyes fixed on the road.

'I am right, then, am I not?' asked Shaw when they had passed Colchester. 'This is about Landis.'

'That's right,' said Wheatley.

'Has there been some development?'

'Development?'

'When you previously visited some days ago to enquire after my health – which was much appreciated, by the way – you said that it was highly unlikely Landis would face prosecution, for reasons of national security.'

'That's right,' said Wheatley through tight lips, his eyes still fixed on the road ahead.

'Then what is the reason for this trip? If there is to be

no prosecution…'

'Mr Shaw,' said Wheatley slowly, as the car's speed topped sixty miles per hour, 'enough questions, eh? Let's just say you won't have to worry about our Dr Landis any more when we get to London.'

'I don't quite understand,' said Shaw. 'But I think I should tell you, Major Wheatley, that I do not intend to let the matter drop. Landis cannot be allowed to get away with what he did. I am not concerned for what he tried to do to me, but for what he may do to others – to innocent people.'

'I've already said, there's nothing you can do,' said Wheatley.

'I can go to the newspapers,' said Shaw. 'Begin a private prosecution, if necessary. Miss Leigh-Ellison, when she has recovered, will I am sure be a willing witness, as will Dr Keating.'

Wheatley slammed his fist on the steering wheel and the car jerked to one side violently.

'Look, Mr Shaw,' he exclaimed violently. 'Why can't you just leave things alone? Why do you have to go barging in leaving a bloody mess for poor devils like me to clear up?'

Shaw was shocked; he had never seen such a display of emotion from the man before.

'May I remind you, Major Wheatley,' he said gently, 'that it was you who asked me to assist in the Ravenswood business.'

'You're right,' breathed Wheatley. 'I'm sorry for shouting at you. I just don't understand what drives you. Keeps you running after danger when you could just have forgotten the names of Landis and Eleanor

Harrington and Ruth Leigh whatever she's called, and just carried on with your life. What is it, some sort of religious thing?'

'My dear Major,' said Shaw, 'I imagine it is the same thing that keeps *you* going.'

'Oh yes, and what's that?'

'A desire to see justice done.'

Wheatley said nothing for the remainder of the journey, and Shaw seemed disinclined to talk to him anyway. He found himself deep in thought. They stopped near Chelmsford for an unappetising lunch in a roadside cafe, and Wheatley watched in embarrassment as Shaw said grace, simply and without self-consciousness, over a dish of egg and chips in a room filled with lorry drivers.

Once they were back on the road, he saw as if it were for the first time the patchwork quilt of the English countryside, gleaming in the spring sunshine, and then the slow trickle of housing developments along the road, until they were deep within the endless, neatly ordered terraces of London.

He listened to the rhythmic roar of the engine, its tone rising and falling in accordance with the gradient of the road; he watched the black-and-white metal signposts count down the miles to central London; 30; 25; 20; 15.

It was if he existed in a huge, well-oiled machine; no, it was more than that; it was as if he, and Reverend Shaw next to him, were integral parts of a vast, beating heart that was the centre of everything in the universe.

He shook his head and lit a cigarette. I must be going off my nut, he thought. Is this what they call seeing the light? It didn't seem like it. Get a grip, man. You're just tired and overwrought, so don't start thinking you're St Paul on the road to wherever it was. You're Major Arthur Wheatley on the road to Redcliffe Mansions, SW1.

As he steered the car through the late-morning traffic, he looked over at Shaw, who had dozed off. He looked peaceful, completely content in his body and mind and trusting himself absolutely to Wheatley's driving. The dashboard clock told him it was 3p.m. An hour to go. He decided he had something to do first.

He pulled the car into a little side street in Marylebone, checking to see if there were any 'no parking' signs, then nudged Shaw awake.

'Are we in London?' asked the clergyman sleepily.

'Yes. Look here, Mr Shaw, I have to check on something. Can you wait here for me?'

'In the car?'

'Yes, if you like. But don't go wandering off, will you?'

'Very well. I have my *Church Times* with me.'

'Righto. See you in about forty minutes.'

Wheatley slammed the car door shut and hurried to the end of the road. He did not know this part of London well but he had seen a bright Underground sign a few yards away, and once inside the station he traced his finger along a map on the wall to check his route. He then bought a ticket and trotted down to the platform.

He emerged from Sloane Square station a short time

later and, turning up his coat collar and pulling down his hat, he eventually found a large, redbrick building near Ebury Square. Redcliffe Mansions.

Noting that there was no porter on duty in the little concierge's office on the ground floor, he quickly padded up the thickly carpeted stairs to the first floor and knocked on a door.

'Dr Landis?' he asked quietly when the door opened a crack. 'I've been sent by Colonel Fellowes.'

The door opened wider, and Wheatley saw Landis for the first time. He suddenly had a vision in his mind of the man bending over Shaw's head with a drill; he had seen that drill for himself when he had visited the ruined hulk of Ravenswood. He shuddered at the memory of the blackened, dripping horror of that basement.

'You're early,' said Landis, who ushered Wheatley into the flat after checking up and down the hallway. 'Where is Mr Shaw?'

'He's nearby,' said Wheatley. 'I'm just doing a bit of a recce.'

'Recce?'

'Recconnaissance, sir. Getting the lie of the land, so to speak. We like to plan things properly in our line of work.'

'Very well,' said Landis, as he closed the door behind them.

'Are we alone?' Wheatley asked, as he looked around at an expensively furnished apartment, with what looked like original old masters hanging from the walls.

'Yes, I've given my man the day off, for obvious reasons,' said Landis as he led Wheatley into a huge, high-ceilinged drawing room with French doors opening out onto a balcony, with views of Ebury Square beyond.

'But I can offer you a drink while you perform your, ah...recce,' he said. 'Whisky?'

Landis crossed to an enormous drinks cabinet and lifted up a heavy crystal decanter.

'No thank you sir,' said Wheatley, though his whole being screamed out for alcohol. 'Don't let me stop you, though.'

He glanced at a long-case clock in the corner which ticked sonorously. It was half past three. Not much time to go now.

'A little early for me, I think,' said Landis, replacing the decanter.

'Just one question for you, sir,' said Wheatley.

'Yes?'

'Is it true what they say about this...procedure of yours? That it...well it sort of destroys a man's soul, so to speak?'

Landis smiled. 'I hardly think that concerns you, Mr...?'

'Wheatley. Major Wheatley.'

'Major Wheatley. Yes of course, I was given your name. I understood your job was to bring Mr Shaw here, not to concern yourself with what happens to him.'

'It's just that this is a bit out of the ordinary for me, sir. I don't often get to meet experts such as yourself. But will this procedure destroy some part of Mr Shaw's faculties? Destroy his faith, sort of thing?.It would be nice to know if I'm helping to make medical history,'

The flattery seemed to work, and Landis smiled

broadly.

'Once I have operated on him, any spiritual sense will be completely removed. He will be as untroubled by matters of faith as a household cat.'

Wheatley saw a gleam in the man's eye, and he began to walk slowly up and down the plush Persian rug by the large fireplace.

'And he will merely be the first. Once my procedure is perfected, countless millions will benefit from it. Think of it, Major Wheatley! A world without the superstitious constraints of outmoded fairy-tales. No more faith, no more doubt, only pure materialism, and pure *obedience*.'

'A race of slaves, eh?'

'In a way. But guided by me, as their benevolent leader!'

'I think I will have that drink after all,' said Wheatley.

'Water?' asked Landis as he poured out the golden liquid into a crystal tumbler.

'Just as it comes, please,' said Wheatley.

Landis smirked self-confidently as he handed the glass to Wheatley, who raised it with a cheery smile.

'Well, here's luck,' said Wheatley as he downed the whisky and placed the glass on a nearby table. He then took his handkerchief and carefully wiped it around the outside of the glass.

He smiled again as he noticed Landis' puzzled expression. 'Yes, here's luck. If Mr Shaw's crowd are right you'll need it where you're going.'

He pulled out the pistol from his pocket and pointed it at the doctor's heart. The silenced gun coughed twice and Landis, with a look of abject horror on his face, was dead before he hit the floor.

At a quarter to four, Shaw looked up with a start as Wheatley entered the car. He had been absorbed in an article on vestments in the *Church Times* and had not noticed the time passing.

'Sorry about that,' said Wheatley as he started the engine. His breath smelled of alcohol and Shaw wondered if the man had furtively visited a public house. Wheatley gave an arm signal from his window and nosed his way out into the traffic along Marylebone High Street. A few minutes later they pulled up at a red-brick block of mansions flats and again, Wheatley asked Shaw to wait in the car.

After some moments Wheatley reappeared, somewhat out of breath. 'I'm sorry Mr Shaw,' he said quickly, 'but I'm going to have to cancel our appointment. Something's come up.'

'But Major Wheatley,' protested Shaw, 'I have sacrificed a large part of the day to assist you. I think that you could at least…'

'Mr Shaw, please,' said Wheatley, reaching across to open the passenger door for Shaw. 'You know I wouldn't do this unless it were absolutely necessary. You'll have to take the train home. There's an underground station just over the other side of the square.'

'But…'

'You can claim it on expenses. Off you go. Look, I'll

explain things later. And please, don't talk to anyone about anything that happened today.'

'But nothing did happen...' began Shaw, but Wheatley cut him off.

'Remember you're working for me, Mr Shaw,' he said politely but firmly. 'I don't want to have to tell you again. Make yourself scarce.'

'Very well,' sighed Shaw, and got out of the car. As he crossed the square, he turned briefly to see Wheatley waving to a black police car which had just pulled up at the kerb. He was tempted to linger, but thought better of it and continued on to the underground station. Within three hours he was back at Lower Addenham, just in time for his meeting.

The following morning at breakfast, Mrs Shaw pushed the *Times* over to her husband and pointed at an article on the second page.

'Isn't that something to do with the Ravenswood affair?' she asked.

Shaw glanced at the headline. 'Doctor shot dead in burglary.'

He grabbed the paper and began to read the article out loud.

'...leading medical researcher Julian Landis was found shot dead at his London residence yesterday. Dr Landis, 45, is presumed to have disturbed a robbery attempt...apartment ransacked...body discovered by porter...police following several lines of enquiry...'

'Are we to consider that good news, Lucian?' asked his wife cautiously.

'"Each man's death diminishes me..."' quoted Shaw, but he felt it ring hollow. Was this some sort of divine justice?

'What was that, dear?' asked his wife.

'Nothing,' said Shaw. 'I must telephone…somebody.'

Before he reached the telephone in the hall, the doorbell rang and he opened it, to find the telegraph boy waiting for him. Shaw tipped him sixpence and hurriedly opened the despatch. It was from Wheatley.

'MEET NETLEY GOLF CLUB 9AM NEXT SATURDAY STOP UNTIL THEN DO NOT DISCUSS CASE STOP AJW'

He crumpled the telegram into a ball and frowned. There was nothing more he could do for a week.

'Come along Mr Shaw,' said Wheatley impatiently. 'If you keep at it like that much longer all the beer in the club house will have evaporated. Try widening your stance a bit.'

Shaw set his legs a little farther apart and putted the ball as gently as he could across the green, but, as he had feared, it overshot the hole by several feet.

Wheatley sighed. He was resplendent in a new off-the-peg golf suit which fitted him moderately well, and he had a jovial, holiday-like air about him. Shaw wished he had not chosen Netley Golf Club as a venue for their meeting. There was no chance of them being overheard, which he assumed was the main reason, but he could not help thinking the man was relishing his awkwardness at the game.

Shaw had only briefly played golf years ago, but after

a while he began to remember some of the technique and, by the time they were halfway round, he was keeping up adequately with Wheatley.

'I think you owe me an explanation about Friday last,' said Shaw.

'Indeed, that's partly the reason for coming here,' said Wheatley. 'I say partly because I rather like this course. It doesn't seem to attract as many of the stuck-up types as the ones closer to London.'

'May I assume Landis' death was not the result of a burglary, as the papers have it?' asked Shaw.

Wheatley paused, and gave an enormous whack to his ball which sent it bounding two hundred yards down the fairway.

'There she goes!' he exclaimed gleefully. 'Officially, it was burglars that did for Landis,' he continued. 'Leastways that seems the most likely explanation. Although some in my department think otherwise.'

'Otherwise?'

'Yes. There's a theory we're working on that it was agents of a foreign power that tried to nab him, you know, to get him to work for them. He resisted and so they shot him, and made it look like a common or garden burglary to hide their tracks.'

'I see.'

'I doubt we'll ever get to the bottom of it,' said Wheatley with a sniff, and took a nip from his hipflask without offering it to Shaw, as the clergyman finally potted his ball.

'May I ask what exactly you brought me to London for?' asked Shaw. 'Was it to meet with Landis?'

'No you may not ask,' said Wheatley. 'Suffice it to say

it was a vital part of the operation when we left Lower Addenham, but circumstances dictated it was no longer required by the time we arrived.'

Shaw fell quiet. He could tell he would get no further with that line of questioning. After a long shot down the fairway, his ball landed several yards from the next hole, and Wheatley shook his head. 'You've hit that ball so much it's practically turned square,' he said.

'I told you I had not played for years,' said Shaw. 'We could just as easily gone for a walk instead.'

'No point in that,' said Wheatley, as they set off down the fairway.

'I should warn you, Major Wheatley,' said Shaw, 'that I do not intend to let this matter drop. Landis may be dead, but there still must be people who assisted him. Who protected him, that is. They must be brought to justice.'

Wheatley stopped and turned to face Shaw, his moustache bristling with anger.

'Now look, Mr Shaw, for once in your life stop playing the saint and martyr. Landis is dead. That's all that matters. One or two people might have colluded with him but they're not important and believe me, you won't get anywhere trying to hold them to account. What's important is that he'll never be able to hurt people like Eleanor Harrington or Ruth Leigh-Ellison again. His notes were destroyed in the fire and his filthy ideas died with him. So I'd like your word, as a gentleman, that you'll let this matter drop.'

Shaw remained silent as they walked to the final hole.

'Very well,' he said finally. 'You have my word.'

'Good,' said Wheatley, 'By the way, how is Miss

Leigh-Ellison?'

'I am pleased to say she is much improved,' said Shaw. 'Keating visited her in hospital and reports that she will soon be well enough to leave. I intend to broker a reconciliation, if I can, between her and her parents.'

'Is that wise?' asked Wheatley.

'Her child is dead. The man who deceived her is dead, and Landis is also dead. There is nobody who can threaten her family now so I see no reason why they should not be prevailed upon to forgive and forget.'

'And I thought my job was difficult,' said Wheatley, shaking his head. 'Thank God I don't have to deal in morality.'

After the final hole had been conquered – Wheatley, of course, was the winner – the two men strolled to the club house.

'The drinks are on me, by the way,' said Wheatley as they sat down at a quiet table in the corner of the little mock-tudor building. 'Got a bit more money coming in now.'

'Indeed, Major Wheatley?'

'Yes indeed. Had a promotion.'

'A...promotion?'

Ahh, that's better,' exclaimed Wheatley as he took a deep swallow of beer from the pint mug that the waiter set before him. 'Yes. It's Colonel Wheatley now. Or at least will be, from next week when it comes through.'

'My congratulations.'

'Colonel!' roared Wheatley. 'On the general staff! I thought I'd been passed over *years* ago! Lor, if my old pa could see me now, he'd laugh fit to bust. But it turns out, Landis getting himself killed was what did it.'

'I don't follow,' said Shaw, as he took a small sip of beer.

'There was the most almighty row, it seems,' continued Wheatley, 'between my chief – we'll just call him "F" as that's what the silly blighter likes to be called – and the Home Secretary. F had made out Landis was his golden boy – him and his brain operations were the last hope for western civilization and so on, and so when he was found dead, F got the blame from the Home Sec. for not keeping proper tabs on him. And he didn't like it one bit when he found out that F had ordered me to…'

He stopped short and looked at Shaw, then cleared his throat.

'Well,' he continued, 'he didn't like a highly irregular order that F had given me. We can do pretty much what we like, but there are limits. Now my old chief, Colonel Raikes, put in a good word for me and blow me if I didn't get made head of department in F's place!'

'My congratulations,' said Shaw.

'F won't be joining the dole queue, of course,' said Wheatley wearily. 'He's walked into another job straight away, like these types always do. They're making him Deputy Governor of the Falkland Islands, wherever *they* are.'

'I am not quite certain,' said Shaw. 'Somewhere near the Antarctic, I believe.'

'Good,' said Wheatley. 'And that's still not far enough away.' He took another swig of beer. 'I still can't believe it,' he chuckled. 'I'll have to get my full regimentals out of mothballs for the commissioning ceremony. And the wife will want a new fur coat now, I'll wager!'

Shaw sat back in the padded leather seat and looked out at the well-manicured countryside of the golf course, with the neat rows of semi-detached villas beyond.

'Major Wheatley,' said Shaw slowly, 'Where exactly did you go when you left me in your car in Marylebone last Friday?'

Wheatley smiled. 'A bit of business that needed attending to. Let's just leave it at that.'

'Is there anything you would like to get off your chest, so to speak?' asked Shaw carefully.

'Well...' began Wheatley, 'what do you think about the lesser of two evils?'

'I'm not sure I follow.'

'Let's say a man did something very wrong. But he did it to stop something even worse happening. Would it still be wrong? Hypothetically speaking.'

Shaw raised an eyebrow, remembering this was the topic he had tried, and failed, to write a sermon about. Somehow he did not feel able to offer any advice.

'Without knowing specifics, it is difficult to comment.'

'I'm speaking generally, of course.'

'Then I would say to this man, examine your conscience – hypothetically speaking, of course.'

Shaw fixed the Major with a steely gaze, and he smiled back.

'*My* conscience is clear,' said Wheatley, ' – as clear as it can be in this business.'

'Very well. But I shall pray for you.'

'Thanks. I daresay I need it.'

'I daresay we all do.'

THE END

Other books by Hugh Morrison

A Third Class Murder (Reverend Shaw's first case)
An antiques dealer is found robbed and murdered in a third class train compartment on a remote Suffolk branch line. The Reverend Lucian Shaw is concerned that the police have arrested the wrong man, and begins an investigation of his own.

The King is Dead
An exiled Balkan king is shot dead in his secluded mansion following a meeting with the local vicar, Reverend Shaw. Shaw believes that the culprit is closer than the police think, and before long is on the trail of a desperate killer who will stop at nothing.

The Wooden Witness
After finding the battered corpse of a spiritualist medium at an archaeological site on the Suffolk coast, Reverend Shaw is thrust into a dark and deadly mystery involving ancient texts and modern technology.

Death on the Night Train
Reverend Shaw is called to the deathbed of an elderly relative in Scotland by an anonymous telegram. Soon he becomes embroiled in a fiendish conspiracy which reaches to the highest levels of the British establishment.

Murder in Act Three
When a cast member is killed during an amateur dramatics performance in the village hall, everyone thinks it was just a terrible accident. Everyone, that is,

except Reverend Shaw. But can he find out the truth before the killer strikes again?

Murder at Evensong
The Dean of Midchester falls to his death from the cathedral gallery during Evensong. Unlike the police, Reverend Shaw is not convinced it was an accident, and is soon drawn into a deadly battle of wits with a merciless killer.

The Tube Train Murder
After aspiring 'talkies' actress Evelyn Parks is murdered on the London Underground, her friend Clarice Thompson becomes dissatisfied with the lack of progress by the police, and begins to look into the case herself – with deadly results.

The Secret of the Shelter
Two children discover a Second World War air-raid shelter half buried in the garden of an abandoned London house. When they go inside, they find they have been transported to the London of 1940 – with no way back.

All Exclusive
A laugh-a-minute romantic comedy set on a tropical island, where British tourists must put aside their class differences to survive a military coup.

Published by Montpelier Publishing
www.hughmorrisonbooks.com
Order from Amazon or via your local bookshop.

Printed in Great Britain
by Amazon